Proie

CHIP MARTIN grew up in California and has lived mainly in London since the early 1970s. He writes criticism under the name of Stoddard Martin and is the author of a sequence of linked novellas, published by Starhaven. He once paid tuition for his higher degree by selling feathered earrings along the beach at St Tropez.

The cover of this book incorporates a portrait by Lovis Corinth of his wife painted at Menton shortly after he had suffered a stroke. It is reproduced by courtesy of its owner.

Proie

a fable

Chip Martin

with special thanks to

Heather Hartley

whose encouragement was essential

ISBN 0-936315-31-8

STARHAVEN, 42 Frognal, London NW3 6AG
in U.S., c/o Box 2573, La Jolla, CA 92038
books@starhaven.org.uk
www.starhaven.org.uk

Typeset in Dante by John Mallinson

As soon as the spirit leaves the white bones, the sinews no longer hold flesh and bones together – the blazing fire consumes them all; but the soul flies away fluttering like a dream. Make haste back to the light, but do not forget all this…

The Odyssey, Book XI,
'How Odysseus Visited the Kingdom of the Dead'

1.

'Your dad would have wisecracked his way through a weekend like this.'

'My dad was politically incorrect.'

'He got away with it.'

'They forgave in that era.'

'They had a sense of humour.'

'Or of cynicism.'

Alexandra had gathered the usual London crowd – the Derrick, Peter and Nigel set, as Dad had called them in his day. You could see how he'd got fed up. France out the window was no more apparent than dabs of post-impressionist colour on the Bonnard nude you passed in the hall on the way into her salon. There sprawled, stood or teetered the chosen. And I might as well introduce us, ghouls though we were, since half wouldn't last out the night.

At the far end of the room where doors opened onto emerald and azure sat a ruddy historian who'd written a fat vol on every imperium since Rome, without ever letting a fact get in the way of a *bon mot*. At his side lounged a contemporary oracle on military strategy, Oxford don, one of whose arms, long paralysed by a stroke, lurched like Dr Strangelove's each time the historian made a joke about 'these South African Jews who run our legal system' or some such – the banter of Thatcherian throwbacks who'd styled themselves Marxist in their hot youth. Making a beeline to bask in their *gloire*, or maybe the precrepuscular light at that end of the room, was a dusky female not far short of them in years. Having begun life in a palace alas gone with the wind, she'd studied at the Sorbonne and been chatted up by Camus before migrating to London after 'the scene changed'. Now she saw virtue in sucking up to *les neo-cons*, as she called them, to get free travel from the 'quality' papers they wrote for, penning profiles of defrocked emirs and wannabe sheiks. In her wake trailed a recent product of Balliol, limp ephebe in puce braces and cordovan loafers with *faux* golden tassels. He had written a thesis on Valéry so exquisite that he'd been plucked straight from the young fogey crowd to pen articles selling the hard *Weltanschauung* of the American Enterprise Institute to the *bien-pensant* English.

'And you don't?' the clever blonde on my left asked, bringing me back to our dangle of conversation.

'I don't what?' – My head revolved.

'Have a sense of cynicism?'

Her mouth, crimson-blue, recalled latex dummies sold on the Tottenham Court Road. A rind round the roots suggested she hadn't always been blonde. Vaguely I recalled her stepping out with a professor of post-Freudianism who now pursued paedophiliac studies at Charles University, Prague. She'd had a mouse dun then; now, hitting fifty, she had to work at it. I wondered if she still gossiped in the back seats of cabs about our hostess's vagina and whether it could excite a man after having given passage at forty to triplets.

'Maybe,' I answered, 'I'm my father's child.'

'In Jamesian disguise?' – She was not without patter. 'Or Gore Vidalian?' she added, provocatively.

The woman on my right purred. I have no idea what the sound meant. Had she choked on one of the damp *hors d'oeuvres* Alexandra served in an attempt to reproduce the atmosphere of a Queen's garden party? Or was it some comment on the blonde's cattiness, of interest to her on the grounds that she'd made her name writing a tome on the threatened status of lynxes in post-Yugoslavia.

The purr came again. 'Excuse me?' I asked, looking round to a bodice that revealed less than intended.

She said, or I thought she did, 'Who *is* your father?'

The blonde retorted, 'You mean you don't *know*?'

'I always think one *should* know,' the tall one observed, 'though the best can never be sure.'

'I'm fond of bastards myself,' I added to this game of battledore and shuttlecock, having not spent teenage in an English public school for nothing. 'But I'm afraid I'm not one of them.'

'Not one of what, or of whom?'

'The blest race of bastards. Wasn't that your question?'

'No. It was "Who was your father?"'

The blonde came to my defense. 'Stop getting at him. Can't you see how he hates being reminded why Alexandra has him on her list?'

2

I doubt the tall one knew how this hit home because she said, 'She invites him on account of his father?'

At which point, the better part of valour seemed to me to relinquish my post between these unattached dames and migrate to the one place in that room where something attracted me truly: sunset gathering out the french doors. But before I could get to it, a guttering alto had inserted, 'Darling! you must tell us – it is so interesting. What did your father do after – '

Fuck my father, I thought, though, having plied adulthood as a supposed gent, I could hardly say so. 'Don't you think it's too beautiful not to go into the garden?' was my substitute.

Les neo-cons were guffawing over some deprecation of frogs as my new companion – let's call her Zabiha – stepped over the threshold beside me. '*Lovely!*' she murmured, extending the vowel out so that you wondered if she were going to break into one of the *Chansons de Bilitis*. 'Rather similar to the prospect from Walid Jumblatt's palace high in the Chouf.'

Was I going to be drawn into politics then? Littoral Lebanon was, as we spoke, being shelled to shards by Israelis.

'It's the colours, the smell, vegetation… Mediterranean Europe and the Levant share in so much… Even by Marseilles, coming down on the train, it assaults you. The Rhône Valley is fine, especially this time of year; but once you enter "the land where the orange tree grows", whatever the rubble, whatever man's devastation, there is no doubt. Our First World northernness just begins to deliquesce.'

Dad might have experienced the sensation, if not used her words.

'Kind of reminds me of L.A. in a Santana,' is what I came back with. 'On a clear winter's day.'

She revolved Kirghiz eyes. They had a look Londoners get when trying to assess if the person they're talking to is beneath the salt. 'Do you mean Los Angeles, darling?' – She pronounced it *angle-less*.

'I'm sorry. I guess you don't know the place. But you did mention Dad. It's why I thought of it.'

The moment was saved by ascent of our hostess. Tall, grand and alert, Alexandra Merton came between us like a scarf floating down on the scimitar of a sultan.

'Antony!' she crooned as if I had dropped out of Shakespeare, this being a riff she'd adopted since the world had learned the *faux*-Elizabethan provenance of my true surname.

Alexandra was one of those fine Englishwomen who believe that to fuss over the least famous person at a party is to identify oneself as having perfect form. Foreigners rarely get this. To spend the precious hour of cocktails networking with a relative nobody might suggest a timidity confirming their own lack of rank. It's the task of outsiders to try to get in, just as it's the duty of insiders to seem to reach out; which precept Alexandra had down to a *t*, as did Zabiha in her reverse way. In an epoch when no one had a thing to say about me except 'he teaches at Birkbeck, or perhaps UC; don of some kind – Eng Lit, I think', the latter had not paid me the slightest attention. Now it was Alexandra who was slightly out of step; because since my real paternity had been bandied around, every Zabiha in town (though she'd never read those books about Dad, I *was* sure) had wanted to chat with me.

We bussed cheeks, Alexandra and I. Then as if leaving half of her silk there to shimmer, she pulled the rest back to drape over the neo-cons, still locked in conspiracy just inside the door. 'Edward!' she crooned to the one, 'Luther!' to the other, swirling her russet around them as if a courtesan's train out of some portrait by Augustus John. It mattered little to her that the one had been continuing on with remarks which to any eavesdropper might have seemed anti-Semitic / anti-frog, nor that the other had just described her raven's wing hair and aquiline nose as denoting 'Huguenot, of Sephardi extraction'. We were the best here: we could say what we liked; we knew who *we* were. No one could have been 'not one of us' and been present. No one would have been present who would have wanted to be.

Zabiha mused on the sunset, 'It's the blue of the sky, darling, the clarity of air, the depth of those greens in the distance... It is even, you see, the pink and white of the oleanders fringing her garden...'

Gold bracelets, brocaded blouse, muslin skirt scarfing down to almost penitential flip-flops... Her brown hair was done up like a petty bourgeoise's. Her French-tinted English spoke of realms further east. Faintly she seemed to exude nostalgia, anger at wars that had cut short a fairytale youth, not-quite-appeased homesickness. Anguish shone in a gaze against fading light, negating before it was re-subsumed by Edward's and Luther's chat, into which she receded once our hostess, having raised a guffaw from that pair, re-trained steps out to us.

'O I'm so weary!' Alexandra breathed; 'I had the oddest dream…' Nipping Zabiha in the bud of our moment *à deux*, she half-whispered: 'It was a party much like this – more of us, though – in her part of the world or perhaps yours, or even here – you know how these things distort. Very jolly at first; then we went for a swim. Three pools were nearby; you and I were standing together slightly to one side. Most were in the first pool; you started for the second, but it was covered with algae and on closer inspection full of large, quite threatening fish. I went towards the third. Coming at me were many more people, more than had been there to begin with. They were dressed rather well, but when I peered into their faces I found all ethnic types, even species. I shook hands with a man in a Valentino jumper who turned out to be a gorilla. An upright tiger in Lagerfeld came up beside him; we were introduced. At last someone I knew and had loved once – young, unidentifiable – arrived pushing a pram or a wheelchair with a hybrid human-crustacean in it. Maimed more than Luther, poor dear, it was all twisted up, yet full of beseeching in its one tiny black lobster eye. I took it in my arms; it seemed very grateful. Everyone was touched by my apparent charity, but shortly – before you arrived, darling, to rescue me – I'd retreated to a corner of the whole scene simply to crouch down and weep.'

I listened to this with the gathering inattention that overtakes you when someone is so tiresome as to tell you her dreams. The effect was not what you'd expect, however. Somewhere in the flow I began to realize how fond I was of this woman, and had been at some level always. A discolouration of eye, unnoticeable in gay chat or from the far side of a room, alerted me to some rare emotion in her. She seemed to be saying that she needed me, *trusted* me. Now, of course I'd been around long enough not to assume that a drop into confidence wasn't part of some more elaborate game – Alexandra had had lovers: Edward and Luther were both in that historical file, as the world knew; her late husband, celebrity playwright and scholar whose pedigree had bought her this house, had been a mainstay of the post-war 'homintern', so called, and it had struck many as faintly miraculous when they'd married, especially given how sexy she was, and could be still. Her production of twins within a few months (a third stillborn) had quickened the general murmur, and a rumour had gone round that some rogue male had played Gabriel at the Annunciation. But the playwright had done Dad like a good, complacent Joseph, and Alexandra had taken to her tasks as wife, hostess and *maman* to the eminent man's sons, as well as promoter of his repute, like the Madonna. Now as his widow she was guarantor of his fame. Nor would anyone have set out for this most sought-after of Provençal *gîtes*, where they had held court to the Great and Good for two decades, without letting *tout* London hear of it first.

'It's all rather exciting, don't you agree?'

A mild tenor interrupted my reverie. Alexandra, having finished her tale, had receded, trailing silk towards the unattached dames, still simpering over some ribaldry at their end of the room.

'Exciting?' – My eyes were blinded by a ray refracting off the white bougainvillea pouring over the west end of her garden.

'To be here. With such famous people.'

It was the young fogey. I returned to focus and saw. Tired of flushing puce for the wit of Edward to Luther, he had come to try his luck with the one other male present. He couldn't have known, or at least have been sure, that I wasn't of his coterie, politically or otherwise.

'Don't you admire them?' he continued, meaning the neo-cons, Alexandra now lost in a scrum with the girls.

'*Nil admirare*,' I breathed, quoting somebody, vision again occluded by the light and its play, soon to be engorged in deep purples.

'You're a cool one,' he smiled, as if flirtatious; and I recalled what I half-knew – that he had been a student of her husband's and was almost the same age as her boys; which led me to wonder why *they* weren't there, though this was forestalled by being blinded once more, now by a ray lazering through thick mimosa.

'That must be the Californian in you,' he mused, and into mind swam other times, other scenes. 'You lived there too, didn't you?'

Again I was pressed back to what they all rated *über alles*: celebrity: fame. '"Too"?' I echoed.

Pastiness turned puce. 'Like your father, I mean.'

He wasn't so dull as to miss irritation. It passed as soon as my sight was restored, leaf eclipsing the ray. 'Dad lived there in one era. By the time I came along, things had moved on, or back.'

'Ah. We tend to forget about time, don't we?' – He was almost apologetic. 'Place isn't everything, is it, when you're identifying the type of a culture?'

You could have liked him, sophomoric though he was. He had a harelip I hadn't noticed at first.

'How do you find it differs?' he added.

'What?'

'L.A., from here?'

I was about to sink teeth into it when Alexandra clapped hands and cried 'Supper!' And by the time we had masticated Salade Niçoise, our world in its orbit was drastically about to change.

Dad had been in his late forties when I'd come along. I was nearing that age at this moment of being half dragged into his game. Between us most of the last century was staked out, also two of its more gaudy locales. The mean streets of his poetic wisecrackings may not have been thought of as as grand as the promenades you passed through to get up here to Alexandra's, but they had long boasted more in money, more in art and more even in 'old family' per square mile than the L.A.-like sprawl down in that galaxy between Menton and Marseilles. And Mom's clan had had no small part in it.

I chewed over these contrasts as we sat at the long table in Alexandra's garden where dinner had been laid. Crickets chattered in odoriferous pines, stars lay thick over velveteen hills. Wafts of warm air and moans of stray dogs on faint breezes colluded to suppress any whir of traffic afar; so that if I had answered the young neo-con's question, it might have been to say that the place seemed more remote and pristine – Southern Cal as Dad would have known it before the boom of oil and industries of war had turned it into the overpaved megalopolis the world liked to think of it as.

But we didn't go there. The mood at the table was frankly rowdy as rosé washed down crème caramel. Some chat re the Near East and current crusade in Iraq morphed via Zabiha's defense of Islam and the condition of women into the condition of men, behind which lurked in all cases but one the condition of sexual relations in middle age. Since my wife's fatal cancer, I'd heard plenty about this, not least from the females collected – Alexandra lamenting how she couldn't 'pull' anymore, Zabiha letting drop that she had 'the body of a sixteen year old'. What the North African servants made of the unattached dames playing virtual Parcheesi over my lap is anyone's guess. But they could hardly have approved of Edward's ribaldry, let alone politics; and Luther's attempt to pet the pertist female rump among them with his non-crippled hand sent up a screech like Zerlina's in *Don Giovanni*.

You might have guessed that this antique hetero foolery would have left our young gay friend *triste* and aloof. But before stars had set, he was lured by the unattached dames via a clump of brush off to a room in a wing of the house where I was not billeted. Music emerged, rather loud I recall; and it was hard to envisage Luther cutting a rug to White Trash or whatever. Alexandra retreated, 'to weep for times passed' she averred, by which we assumed her late husband; and I was left to trade scabrous remarks with Edward as Zabiha weighed up whether to ally herself with me or continue to pay court to a chap whose views were in flat contradiction to ones she was too self-interested not to suppress. I wandered to bed finally. An urge related to too much *marc* made my sandals slow in front of our hostess's door; but nostalgia for Mom and her years of disgruntled widowhood after step-dad had died (her third husband, though hardly last lover) failed to send up a flame sufficient to halt them.

Bittersweet imagery lending new motion, up stone steps they tapped, leading me eventually to a room from which you could see light almost nowhere. Provençal night with its thick scent and soft sounds wound in, interrupted only by Edward's grumbles below and a vague twang of hard rock in the distance. Should I have gone there? Though no longer thirty, I was not a day older than the 'girls'. They might have had me – our young fogey too, if present. But then a cry came – Luther, I supposed, hand up some new skirt; on which image I faded into Dad's sort of disgust, wrenched the duvet off the mattress and lay down on it almost cold… That's how it was.

I awoke now and then, both wishing and hating to be the one thing our world no longer allows you to be: old. I was depressed, virtuous and *mirabile dictu* had a wet dream, the face of a Moroccan Luther was groping somehow in it. That sort of thing is always a waste, the body's joke or revenge, though not unusually strapped to some guilt-edged delight. But here in the chill before dawn, and at my age, it meant only get up, stagger off to the loo, wipe the mess clean and go back to trying to get in an hour or two more, so as not seem too greyed-out by whatever sordid veneer had been left by the unbidden phantasm that had caused an unwelcome surge in the first place.

Dad, forgive me. I was not so fastidious as you. Anyhow, it was the sun what done it. Through blue shutters it snuck, they being no more able to hold it back than my fist had an a-chronic rush. So I gave in, tumbled upright again, went over and un-louvered them to a blaze.

Such vitality out there! Helion in his chariot just breasting a ridge of the faraway Alpes-Maritimes – a true triumph of life... Gold and red-orange – colours I'd loved since earliest picture-dreamings... but here came an errant thought: how could I deal with them *now*? Wasn't I too worn out, too flat mediocre to handle such *gloire*?

Something had gone wrong. Gorgeousness scalded the ridge. A scent hit my nostrils; the rays through the branches seemed to be jetting flame. Yes, there *were* flames. And smoke was here too, swirling *grey*... The villa was burning.

From below rasping hisses... I leaned out to see crimson chew flowers and vines. Over a garden wall tongues of flame licked, as if someone had laid out a meal for them. Up the far wing they slurped, seeking out bits of timber between clumps of stone. Impelled by a breeze that had come up in the night (promise of Santana – sorry, Mistral) they slapped at the windows, darted between cracks, flicked bits of plaster, spat, keened, guffawed. Soon fire was roaring and any scream in a nightmare subsumed in its rising quavers of heat.

Smoke billowing turned the world impenetrable. Was that Zabiha coming in from dawn prayer? Were those the young servants rolling up mats, having knelt like worshippers beside camels in deserts to send up praises to Allah at earliest light? In truth, I saw nothing – not even panic in a mind's eye. Someone had done something, because the next thing I knew I was waking again out of a dream, only this time a dry one, as brittle as old sticks.

The bed I lay in was as white as cheap porcelain. A sister moved at its foot, hair ebony, done West African style. She too was white, except for brown arms and face. Clipboard in hand, she loomed up to peer down. I sensed gauze then and realized that my right side, anyhow the best part of it, was fried darker than her.

2.

Alexandra sat at the heart of her flagstone patio. Behind her lay a tapestry of scorched gorgeousness. Not all the bougainvillea had been crisped; some green even managed to bud out of end-of-the-world black. Eden, it seemed, could remain a hope beyond the apocalypse.

'Darling.' – She stood and came towards me, hands extended. 'Have they patched you up well? Let's see.'

She inspected my face, taking maternal persona. This fell away into scents of Chanel, Hermès over taffeta or some fabric flowing like a veil down a statue of Hera, crossed with Veroushka on a catwalk.

'Perfect,' she decided, leading me by those hands to a recliner at the east end of her terrace. The wing of the house we had slept in, I saw, had escaped with no more than a singeing.

'How so?' I enquired, perfection having little to do with what I was feeling just then.

'Your allure as ruin far exceeds your attraction as normal man.'

If anyone else had said this, one of the unattached dames for example (their aura still lurked), I might have taken it awry. But she seemed to exude a higher authority then: something oracular, finished in an aesthetic sense. Years passed into timelessness as we sat in the shadow of a vine, whose grapes had been ripened by flame.

Her eyes were obscured behind designer lenses. They mirrored me back distorted against yellow fields.

'What did the police say?' I asked.

'Obvious. Land development scam.'

'You don't believe that?'

'Do you mean do I suspect that one of my Moroccans did it? Edward thinks so. He maintains that the police are covering up out of fear of copy-cat terrorism.'

I turned it over. 'Edward would. How is he?'

'Not a scratch. Back in Holland Park. He'll eat out on it for ages.'

'And milk it for all its anti-frog worth?'

'Edward remains Edward.'

We considered.

'Zabiha?' I asked.

'Left for Beirut soon as they released her. "Brushed by death, darling, one realizes what in life truly matters… I need to see the hammams again and the fountains; to hear the muezzin cry."'

'And escape inevitable suspicion from Westerners?'

'There's that too. O, I do feel for her.'

We imagined the scene.

'Were they very heavy?'

'No more than you'd expect. The fact that she wasn't in the house at the time did look odd.'

So she *had* been out at prayer, as I'd guessed, or at least for a walk in dawn gloaming.

'How were they to your Northern Africans?'

'Beastly. But Zabiha, after decades in London, is less used to it.'

A summary of police action trailed into layered tones of Provençal morning. The sun was not high and to the south, where we faced, a ladder of clouds decorated boyish blues towards St Tropez.

'The others?' I asked, to get the worst over.

'Terrific kerfuffle. Don't die in France, darling. The inconvenience to one's friends!'

This was not said heartlessly. Nor were her details about form-filling, flap over coffins, fury from Luther's wife – widow now – as well as difficulties in locating the significant others of others. 'Our young man,' she concluded, 'paid a price dearer than he could have imagined for his lapse into hetero rumpy.'

It seemed lurid. 'Was that what was on?'

'Darling, those girls… I only invited them to appease Luther and Edward. A pair of old *roués* trying slip through my door at three in the morning is not what I fancy. But the young man…'

We hesitated over the scene. Anyhow I did, and began to wonder how Edward had managed to resist temptation – surely not via the 'sixteen year old' attractions of Zabiha?

A transparent pearl meanwhile slipped under my hostess's lenses. 'He was hardly older than my boys,' she murmured, before being interrupted by a clatter of stones up the drive.

We turned and saw out of the poplars emerge a grey Deux-Chevaux, ghost of the late 1960s. Tissue to nose, Alexandra got up and, as gears shifted and racket died next to her long, new Citroën and my smaller rental one, crossed what was left of a patio to greet a pair of North Africans, male and female, who had served on the night of the party. They chatted, and I let thoughts rove. Inconsequently they arrived at the topic of how lucky I'd been. Someone, her or these two, had located my wallet unburnt, with driver's license in it, though not passport. Resistance of plastic meant that I'd been able to acquire transport in France, though not yet back to London. The vice-counsel in Nice would be working on that; for the moment I was stuck here, condemned to wondering what had happened in life, why and where it had left me. I won't clog this narrative with where I had been: the past could return as future demanded. Now the near present was too full of incident to prevent me from indulging in what all of *them* would've wanted to ask even more: about Dad.

It occurred to me as she led the newcomers into what remained of her kitchen that, if he'd been here, he might have smelled a rat. To him her Chanel mixed with *herbs de Provence* may have muffled some less pleasant odour. Were these North Africans agents of hers in some way? Did the torching of the house have to do with some clichéd, virtually Southern Californian insurance scheme? What were the financial facts of the case? Her husband had been rich – we all took that for granted – but was it so? Are the apparent rich rich really ever? In a world of illusions, that world Dad knew so well, was any 'old money' not sustained by a general falsity? There was me, of course: I could get by on what Mom had been left from her dad, as well as what trickled from *my* father's estate – royalties her lawyers and a step-dad's graft had wrested from the Hollywood types who'd grown fat on his tales. My battles had been fought by a previous generation; I was taken care of in some modest way – so modest that few could see it, especially in contrast to folk with the chic style and lavish hospitality of Alexandra. But what was the truth about her?

'They've come to help me clear up,' she explained of the Moroccans, returning to her recliner.

'Have you decided what you're going to do?'

'A ruin looks better than one of these contemporary "villas".'

'So you're not going to let them drive you away?'

'I'm unconvinced by the land developer theory. In any event, no. This is where *I* intend to die.'

She said this with finality. I could only counter, 'Not soon, I trust.'

'That remains to be seen. But they, whoever *they* are, won't drive me off, no.'

So that was it. No more pearls slid under dark lenses. A tensing of skin over bone in a cheek seemed to say that what she said would be backed up by the force with which she had said it.

I shifted. Time to go, find a hotel, some perch to idle on and sort out what this external *crise* meant for me. But 'Stay a minute, darling', she added, 'I have a favour to ask…'

So there arrived my mission. I was the one chosen to go find her sons and tell them what had happened.

'Why me?' I wondered once she'd finished with what little she was willing to fill in about it.

'Why not? You're a hero.'

'Hero? How so?'

She described how I'd managed to get one appendage burnt and half a face. I recalled not a bit.

'You mean I went in there to pull out the others?'

We gazed at a spot where her west wing had been. Now it was merely the rind of a char.

'There were screams; you heard and ran to help. You hadn't got through the door before that beam came down on you. Hanan' – the female of the North African couple – 'and I pulled you loose.'

I'd been concussed, it was true. Her tale was credible, yet her spin on it overly flattering. 'Your dad would have been proud of you,' she almost added but, having a sense of what went too far, if not always the restraint to apply it, held back.

'That doesn't sound "heroic".'

'Don't be shy, darling. I've always known you had more in you than that effete exterior puts out.'

I raised a brow. 'She that bestoweth taketh away?'

'Well, if you won't accept praise...'

The phrase had no play in it, only annoyance. She lapsed into silence, and the breeze purred. A mower or farm vehicle chuntered away at a distance. Occasional cracks or bangs came from where the Moroccans ransacked. Two small boys had once clamoured for nursery food in there, I mused, the image incongruous next to what faced me now: *maman* as *grande dame*.

'Why me?' I repeated.

She just stared. Jaw set, the bones in the cheek had gone stark. An eagle depleted, searching for prey... in that pose she looked ugly, not even a *jolie laide,* though the belt around her waist – wide patent leather – cinched a form that would not be allowed to go slack.

'They don't have a father. They won't speak to me – we needn't go into why. They must be told what's happened, especially James. Go to him first – I'll give you a name. Rafe can come later. He can answer the questions I see in your face, if he feels like it.'

More silence. A nerve in the cheek twitched, as if she needed a drink. Nodding, I took a step back.

'Well?' she concluded, tipping her specs, beneath which aqueous sadness seemed to swim. The eyes were too proud to beseech, though you knew – and knew she intended it so – beseeching was in them.

'I'll be happy to see them. Tell me where you'll be, so I can report.'

She flicked a curl towards the house.

'Here?'

'I already said: I won't be driven off, no. I'll turn to ash, like those dear innocents, before I'll let them do that to *me.*'

3.

An image of an Orthodox girl dancing down some dusty West Bank street came to mind as I drove – news on the radio rehearsing some clip on BBC days before. So... could the police have been right? Forest fires had been set here the previous summer; north Africans had been blamed by the National Front, but everyone else said it was developers. 'J'accuse!' café conspiracy-theorists muttered, about this gang, that mafia – Comoro, the Russians, Niçoises, Corsicans, the Pope's armies, Simon de Montfort…

I came through Le Cannet too quick to dwell on Bonnard and dropped into Cannes below Le Suquet. It was the day after Festival ended. Two in the afternoon and the populace, knackered, was siesta-ing away former delights. A build-up of months had burst like the loins of an ex-con in a brothel; now all was tatter and tear-down. Along the Croisette yesterday's hawkers and guys doing charcoals of you-as-a-star – vanished. A few tired workmen up lampposts were pulling down posters; neon still flashed above the wedding-cake of the Carlton and mirrored glass of Noga Hilton. Grand hotels on the day-after being the dullest of haunted houses, I turned into Rue d'Antibes, drove to Place Lamy, parked and set out to find the nearest rest under two stars.

There are always rooms in France smelling of late nights in sad cafés. Once they were the domain of humpbacked widows with poodles, now it was all dusky men with an eye to football on TV; but the feel was the same. You were free here. You could be a failure, a pervert, Henry Miller *manqué* or Simenon's gumshoe; just don't be too rich, man, unfriendly or a fool, and you'll be left in *tout confort*. Pay your bill, eat your croissant, drink your not-so-good-anymore café in the a.m. and step out. You're a free man – freer than almost anywhere on earth.

I checked in. The bed had a lump. The room reminisced on an old slapper's sweat. Down in the street every mo-ped and white van sent up its racket of woe; but that is a certain kind of France. I napped until five, then got up to go promenade to the harbour. The guy at the desk looked at me as if my face weren't half-bandaged, or as if half-bandaged faces were the style of the month. Maybe they were, after the Festival. I grinned crookedly – there's a freemasonry among losers – and sauntered out into palm fronds.

Port towns are boats, but even without them Cannes is one of the best on that coast. The bluff of Suquet and colours of the old town reminded you there was life here before moving pictures moved in or the Victorians started to buy up sea-front real estate. Larger than

St Tropez, less artificial than Monaco, more integrated into a real city than Antibes, Cannes plays second fiddle only to old Nice, with its *soupçon* of Genovese corsairs. A last outpost of *vraie France* before Liguria begins, its Îles des Lérins offshore protective and near, Cannes seems familiar, almost cosy and not just for show. In short, I was not unhappy to be there.

The sea shimmered bright as a corrugated roof, silhouetting petits bourgeois retaking the trottoir. A few over-baked types in clothes light and skin alligatored swivelled a lecherous eye while tugging pink-bowed pooches recalling Mom's later days in Palm Springs. I stepped around one, male at a guess, stooping to scoop up a driblet, plastic-bag involuted to purpose. Then I was into the crowd of skate-boarders and petty-doper teens who congregated around a littered wedge of green announcing approach to the Palais.

This angular construction of pre-fab and glass made you feel almost sorry for France. That her most important cultural event should take place in it suggested the fall from grace Mom had always referred to when explaining why she had never gone back after dragging Dad off on honeymoon to Paris. Mercifully, the port was but two steps away. It was where I was headed.

At a long, low capitanerie I asked a question, got a shrug. It seemed a setback – was my face *une problème*? In the benign sun, even shadowed by hill, I hardly cared. Was there any reason I shouldn't take all the time in the world to locate the name Alexandra had given?

Not far down the quay, an old guy was staring up from a tub. It seemed like an invitation, so I said, 'Monsieur, je vous en prie: est-ce que vous connaissez Loretta Boyar?'

He was tall, slim, Gary Cooper aged. 'Loretta?' he mused in vintage American, apt to the rôle. 'Find her over there, th' far end – past where they're takin' down those crap tents.'

I nodded and Dad surged in mind. Recalling a day before he had vanished, I was in Catalina again with him and his friend Red Noorgaard. I couldn't have been more than three / four at the time, but memory of it was vivid. The semi-tropical breeze, the otherworldly light – flashes brought back years of wonder over what *his* life had been like before Mom had entered the scene.

Emerging out of the shadow of Suquet, I passed scores of yachts harbouring vagrant dreams. Filing the old timer to one side of the mind, I made a note to look him up later. His boat hadn't been that much of a tub after all, though black-hulled and squat. Its glinting brass and waxed wood spoke of days before Earth had been overtaken by plastic, which is what I was heading into now.

The east side of port was all headgear of radar, satellite dishes, helipads. Only a handful of boats were content to rest in old glories like his. From the deck of one a young man appeared to be tracking my progress, so as I came up alongside I called, 'You know of a lady named Loretta Boyar?' – His head ticked. He seemed to be looking beyond or around me, so I tried again: 'Know where I might find a gal goes by the name of Loretta Boyar?'

He was eighteen or nineteen, perfectly slim, hair with a curl to it, light-tinged. On closer inspection he was shocking to look at: a model for some latter-day Praxiteles. The skin wasn't bronzed, but the eyes, round as moons, held the timelessness you imagine to come from years of gazing at nothing but sea. Mine involuntarily fixed on them; they didn't fix back, though a weird awareness seemed to lurk. Still with no answer, I waited. Then abruptly he howled 'No!' and, raising a hand, fingers splayed, gestured me off.

It wasn't hostile, only bizarre. He seemed to have dropped from some other planet, this kid. So was Ariel *his* father, I wondered, feeling oddly drawn. – 'No Loretta!' He repeated the gesture.

I was still staring, tracing a shade of a smile, when a second figure appeared on deck beside him. This one was dressed in all white too: cream or the colour of linen. Pleats in her shorts and a pinch at their waist recalled days when such fabric had been *de rigueur* for all yachties: get-ups like this with short-sleeved knit shirts unbuttoned at collar. 'What is it, Jimmy?' she asked.

The boy didn't answer but, as if appeased by her tone, turned back to what he'd been doing before I'd arrived: polishing the rails in long, regular sweeps. 'Can I help?' she added down at me.

'I'm trying to find someone named Loretta Boyar.'

She seemed to assess what might have disturbed him. 'I'm Loretta,' she stated. 'Who are you?'

I took my time in answering, assessive too. Tall, slim, not so gold-tinged as he was, she wore dark glasses half over brown eyes. Her face was tanned, her hair a weave of fawn colours, not long. A touch masculine, though not hard, she seemed possibly on the far side of thirty, maybe a decade short of my age.

I told her my name, using step-dad's as per norm. Adding who'd sent me made her glance to the boy, or young man as he was, to determine if his concentration were re-set. Polishing, polishing, he made a weird keening music under the breath. She asked:

'What does *she* want?' meaning Alexandra.

It was neutral, not hostile. Still, it seemed to hold me at arm's length, so I snapped, 'Can't you at least invite me on board? I'd rather not shout from down here in the street.'

It wasn't a street really, though cars could pass through if they had permits – riverains, big wigs. She looked to the gate they would enter before responding *sans* word by lowering a plank. Up I stepped.

The deck was a marvel: wood of the warmest hue and supplest feel under the sole of a flip-flop. Polishing, polishing had rendered it like the parquet of some old bibliophile's den. I wanted to see more, but she offered no invitation. 'And?' was all she came out with.

'Not even a cold drink on a hot day?'

'I'm sorry, we don't have time. We're expecting guests. We have to cast off as soon as they show.'

Who she was expecting appeared almost before she spoke. Sound first – a whir at the back of my head – sight second, flaring into her lenses. I turned to take in three late-model Lancia touring-cars, classic-grilled, Rossini grey. Smoothing to a bollard next to the mooring, the drivers' doors opened and out stepped men in sharp suits to pop doors in the rear. From these emerged a blonde movie-star whose name I won't mention – it's too famous; a PA or factotum in tan pantsuit with female cousinage to what the drivers had on; last but not least a small guy resembling a toreador, knot of hair at the base of an ovoid skull, olive skin and a light-weight brown suit sausage-ing the torso. He looked to Loretta as doors syncopatedly shut. Ticking an eye at me, he seemed to want explanation. But just then the wild child or young god or whatever he was ran down deck towards us, reverie disturbed. With arm out and hand motioning as before, he cried,

'No! Not coming aboard, no!'

'Jimmy reminds us,' Giovanni Liskau would observe a half-hour later, 'of what is truly important.'

By then the world-famous designer would be gazing into sunset gathering. We were in his cabin, I seated across from him on built-in, suede-covered benches. Loretta had been dispatched to run the ship. Before she'd able to justify my presence, he had apparently gleaned something useful, because he'd cut in,

'We run over to Monte tonight – the brother is there. You wish to speak with him? It may be your chance.'

The actress had vanished to whatever lurked below – elegant playboy's stateroom, I assumed. Others had set off to do whatever they did, the Lancia boys soon in outfits as sported on the pages of *GQ*. The factotum had disappeared forward to use phone, fax and email in a cabin that doubled as an afloat office.

'He reminds us,' the man mused in an accent as smooth as the vermouth he poured, 'that civilization is a construct fashioned by man, but out of his control. It is a fabric we weave, cut and shape. Sometimes the result can be so fine that it makes even more glorious the most beautiful bodies Nature may provide. At other times it turns out grotesque and invites us to tear it to shreds.'

He knew Alexandra, he said, and about the fire – *Nice Matin* had reported it the following day, when I'd been in hospital. It bemused him evidently when I told him why she'd sent me:

'To inform Jimmy?' – it was how they referred to this one of her twins. 'Nobody can make *him* understand such a thing, not so he can see it. Perhaps Loretta only, or his brother, if he should wish.'

I sipped. He sipped. We contemplated our subject, who loitered at stern. It was not so dark yet that all colour had faded, and the sky around him was glowing. Soon he would be haloed in infra-red; then all would turn black as coal. What he resembled was too bright and round-faced to recall his mother. Having thrown off a line at Loretta's command, he stood gazing down. She'd turned on the throttle; we moved into the channel; he studied the pools progress made.

'The boy's autistic,' Liskau observed. 'It's her cross to bear, Alexandra's. She married a genius – desperate for kids: even the most glamorous women can be at that age – there is one on this boat even now. She took drugs, hormones; performed every trick. Did you know her then? Unless you did, you might never have guessed. She's clever, that one – can mask anything, to almost anyone.'

I turned it over. 'But not you?'

'My dear man, I'm no breeder. They can trust me, especially if I'm their couturier. Especially if I'm the one who gave them their start in the first place.'

'Alexandra was your protégé?'

'The plot thickens. Why would she chose someone to come on this mission who knew her so poorly?'

I had no response to this, nor to his quizzical smile. Whatever he made of my mug in present condition, what I made of his was that it seemed like a handsome, aging ferret's. Not that I'd spent hours gazing into the eyes of such beasts, but that's what came to mind.

As it did, a peach moon rose behind it. This revealed itself shortly to be the face of the actress. Her flat form rose underneath, nondescript in the plainest of sweatsuits. The famous thin hair was pulled back in a pigtail like Liskau's, but on her it did not look chic.

Seeing my eyes move to the rustle, the designer turned. 'Ah, bella... Feeling stronger? We can take supper here, no?'

Flopping on a cushion, she didn't look at him. Not looking at me either, she asked, 'Where's the boy?'

He tutted. 'Nervous, my sweet?'

'"Nervous"?' – She glared at him, rather savagely, I thought, though you could hardly say in that half-light. 'You know, Joe' – so she called him, inaptly, lighting a fag – 'not everyone regards autism as some mild eccentricity.'

'I'm impressed you should take such an interest.'

'Well I'm not just a pretty face, am I?'

'No one would have said so.'

'I'm trying to get this straight. You don't, like, just keep him around as an accessory, do you?'

'Accessory? to what?'

'O for fuck's sake, be serious.'

Liskau's teeth gleamed. 'Not fond of the word, Schatz, especially before guests; though from your lips, some might find it enticing.'

Glancing at me, she muttered 'Sorry' and reached out the hand not occupied with smoke. We touched tips. Hers belonged to a mortal appendage, or reasonable facsimile. A degree chillier maybe.

'Accessory,' she repeated. 'Everyone knows what an accessory is, Joe – like that watch on your wrist, or that earring. The handbags you get rich off of.'

'Let's not talk shop now, please.'

'O for fuck's sake!'

I wondered what to make of her in the flesh. Celebrity being what it is, it was hard not to disparage. She looked far from glamorous as she spat at him, 'So?'

'So what, mein liebe?'

'Where is he?'

'Where is who?'

'The boy! damn you. The fucking boy!'

'My darling. You are obsessed.'

'No.' – She inhaled on her fag as if it were rare weed. 'Just interested, as I should be.'

'As you should be. As we all might be. As this man is in his way.'

Swivelling, she took in the half-and-half of my face. 'What's that s'posed to mean?' stubbing the fag. 'What's happened to him?'

'To whom?'

'To "whom"?' She jerked her head round: a pumpkin, not pretty. 'To "whom"?! Are you kidding me? Are you having me on? Don't go "to whom"-ing me at a moment like this. I've trusted you with the most precious thing in the world to me and you sit there "to whom"-ing? O for fuck's sake!' she repeated for a third time and, rising, flounced off to wherever it was she had come from.

The boat slipped past harbour lights, into the stretch towards the Îles. Did it strike me that I should get off then? A room in a flea-bag can sometimes be preferable to hysterical grandeurs – often, maybe. Which put me in mind again of Dad... What if he hadn't copped it in a shoot-out at Fifth and Flower like they said, but just slipped out of town before Mom's martinis and menopausal maunderings had turned life into something he didn't care to go on with? That's how it had happened for my step-dad, RIP, though I'd only observed from afar. Doubtless I'd been lucky they'd sent me to Le Rosay, even though I'd protested. Who in that era would have wanted to give up California for Europe? I'd just started puberty; Easter week in Palm Springs was at its height – influx of bikers, hot-rodders, ho-dads and surfer chicks down-n-dirty, along with frat guys from Berzerkly. Poof! I was off into the chilly mountain fastness, an all-boy régime, demands to learn French, German and reckon my status among an international élite. What would Dad have made of it had he stuck around? How would he have cared for me if he'd sweated it out? Would he have wisecracked his way through it, like the rest of the fallen world he'd lived in, or might he have taken a thing seriously at long last? given up the tactic of just mordantly observing and tried to do something positive, some-thing to help someone, this someone he had created?

Before I'd descended too far into brown meditations, I brought eyes up and, peering into the no longer shaded ones of my host, tried to pick up the thread. But he'd dropped it too, evidently. The dark of his pupils was no longer focused on mine, but beyond or around them, over or through, making me revolve to take in what they were gazing at: Loretta at the wheel, a classic 18th century job, cradling its sculpted handles as she eased the craft out, and Jimmy, who'd escaped from his trance at the stern to drape himself over her like some great cat, stretching an arm up, inclining his Apollonian curls into hers.

'Such is love,' Liskau murmured; 'though all is not how it seems… There is love here too, whatever our Oscar-nominee thinks. Look.'

I was looking. He was looking. Were we both longing? As we did, Jimmy peeled off and, Loretta contented – appeased, you might say – drifted off towards us in his not-quite-of-this-world way, a motion so light that plimsolls hardly touched deck, a look so distracted and inward that, if it caught yours, did so only in quick, furtive glances, followed by flashes as of insight or repulsion. Now I'd been in his view long enough, it seems, because he passed me by with no sign of dis-content and came to rest next to his protector, settling in beside him so naturally that you might've imagined them lovers.

The designer may have been thinking along similar lines because, once an appeased look had crossed *his* features, he was quick to repeat: 'It is not what it seems…' And after a spell of holding the boy close, he added, 'You must tell Alexandra in your way not to fret. He is looked after here; we know what to do.' – Which phrase, uttered in what was now inky darkness, sliced off the topic. And with a motion like Poseidon brandishing a triton, he brought his crew up on deck.

Glassed candles were lit, the cabin set for supper. It was a balmy evening, so aft doors were left ajar: we could sit half-in, half-out as it were. Shortly we were joined by the factotum – a brittle East Coast type, Vassar, Wellesley – and actress re-emerged. Jimmy wandered off as lightly as he had come; Loretta stayed at the helm; the others, though present, seemed invisible as they went about their normal *va-et-vient*. Liskau fell silent as the two women argued – that is, one asserted and the other challenged, their subject being Condoleeza Rice and Hillary Clinton and who might become the first female President. I watched the coast pass – 'fairyland', as my old mom might have called it: the lights of the Îles, Golfe Juan, Cap d'Antibes. Did I bother to think what a strange position I was in? Was it possible that injury had left me a bit tetched? Vaguely, I recalled a room back in Cannes where I'd napped for an hour. Was I likely to get back to it? What had I left there? Was the rental car safely parked?

'She's a bitch,' snipped the one.

'Least she's not an Oreo cookie,' the other, and so on, until Liskau, bored stiff, interrupted:

'Ladies, ladies… Who would look better in the line of suits I'll make for her? That is what signifies.'

The factotum trilled a high-pitched little laugh. The actress reverted to 'O for fuck's sake, be serious.'

'Darling, I'm a pragmatist,' he retorted. 'You two are the ones flailing feathered boas in air.'

The facto trilled again.

'Whatever that means,' sarked the actress. 'Where's the boy?'

'Do be less impatient.'

'I have a window of two days.'

He didn't like it. In the glow you could make out a curling lip.

'Omigod, I almost forgot!' cried the facto. 'Have to call the harbour before we get there… Sorry!' – She scampered off.

The actress lit a new fag and was about to spit some further intemperance at Liskau when he turned to me and said, 'It may be too late or too early for you to reach them when we get there. You may use my apartment to rest.'

'I thought we were going to use your apartment,' the actress objected, before I quite understood.

'Better stay on the boat.'

'Why?'

'Someone might see you.'

'You mean paparazzi?'

'That would be fine for me, but n.g. for you. Disruptive.'

'What?'

'Don't be childish. Shifting to the apartment.'

'You mean – '

'Basta!' he murmured, pinning her with a look that I couldn't fathom; but she could.

'I'll put this gentleman there,' he said, genial again once she had clammed up. 'He may need a wash before going to see the brother.'

'What "brother"?'

'Liebe, you are *so* inquisitive.'

'You would be too if you were me.'

'But I'm not. Nor unlike millions would I wish to be. You forget that I'm a celebrity too, only I have fewer problems with it. I'm a man; I'm in charge; I'm not ruled by forces I cannot control.'

At this point from below came a sound like a moan. And whatever monster it came from, left unexplained, cleared the table of Liskau. After some seconds of studying me, the actress dematerialized too.

Could I blame her? I was no pretty sight. Had I been ever? Someone may have thought so, once; but that was history now. In middle age it's only money that attracts, fame or some equivalent power. Dad had had the one: it's why Mom had gone for him, despite her revered papa's reputed hundred mill. Giovanni Liskau had another, vastly incomplete. And then there was Jimmy.

He was the source of the moaning, of course: of that you could be sure. He too was the reason no one came back to me soon – not for the rest of the distance to Nice, as it happens.

What had gone on down there? – 'It's usually nothing,' Loretta explained, she being the one who surfaced at last, wheel handed over to some Lancia guy (we weren't under sail yet; it was windless; she could afford a break). 'This time it was dinner. They gave him caviar blinis, but naturally he wanted kaiserschmarm.'

'Naturally,' I echoed, recalling some trial of Rosay privilege.

'Terrible stuff. But he's only a kid… Gianni has him distracted. They're showing him one of her tamer videos.' *Her* being the actress.

'Not *The Cat that Walked Backwards*?'

'I said one of her tamer ones.'

We grinned. At least I hoped she could tell I was giving back the visual equivalent of her friendly tone.

'You must be wondering what the hell you're into.'

'It has occurred to me there may be things I don't get.'

'Things I don't either. May be best not to ask.'

'Is that a warning?'

'Or confession of weakness.'

'You don't look weak to me.' – It was pitch black.

'Of or inadequacy,' she amended.

'You don't look inadequate either.'

If she blushed, I can't say. Fortunate, really. She couldn't tell how my unrehearsed words had brought blood to *my* cheeks. In truth, I liked her – you have to be drawn to someone. In the film biz, it's the techies everyone goes for. I knew that from my summers in L.A., those precious escapes from the grey school they'd sent me to after Rosay. Dad's town had held nostalgia for me ever since: a sweet spot of home and adventure. Driving out Sunset to the Palisades would eternally float in the mind, as evocative as this stretch of coast slipping past under its spangle of stars.

'That's Villefranche up there,' she murmured, reading my thought, or possibly avoiding it. 'It's the deepest harbour in this part of the Med. One of the prettiest too.'

I wanted to ask her… what, I'm not sure. She seemed to have

answers, despite what she didn't say. In her flat, what-you-see-is-what-you-get manner, there was some lure to appeal to an autistic boy. Dogs have instincts; humans do too; only civilization occludes them. And as Liskau had opened by saying, Jimmy was perhaps better placed than most to sense who or what was important.

Loretta knew things, but before she was willing to enlighten me about them, or on why Alexandra had sent me to find him, and her, she was up again, trailing, 'Got to get back to the wheel... Gianni'll join you before long for a nightcap.'

So I was left alone again, even more so this time. So I started to drift. The rock of the boat, which hadn't struck me at first, vague sense of physical release that comes on you at sea... I was ready to dream. Maybe I was doing so already when a new voice interrupted:

'I have your agenda.'

This one, also female, had a scrape to it.

'Agenda?' I guttered.

'You do have a purpose in being here, don't you?'

'Is that an existential question?' – I pulled myself up.

'We'll get on better if you don't try to be cute.' – It was the facto-tum. 'I don't appreciate spanners being thrown in the works.'

'A spoke might get broken?'

'Cut the Chandler crap, guy. It's so last century.'

I might have guessed that this third of his nymphs would have required her moment. She too was slim, though crimp-featured, flat-chested. If the actress had previewed descent into mortal plumpness by middle-age and Loretta ascent into sublime androgyny, this one seemed destined to take on an essence of isolate fury.

'Your agenda is as follows: one of our men will take you when we get to Fontvieille; you can stay at GL's till ten/eleven. Later, and you may miss him.'

'Miss whom?'

She made a sound suggesting I was a contemptible prat. It wasn't the first time anyone had done so; still, it was poorly designed to win friends or induce affection.

'Sam Mazandaran. Who else would I mean? Prince Ranier?'

'He dead.'

'Gosh, you *are* up to date.'

'Up to last year's newspapers. Who's Mazandaran? one of the Russkies who torched Edmond Safra?'

She paused long enough to make you wonder if Langley VA lurked somewhere in the background. 'It was the male nurse,' is what she came back with.

'Who?'

'The man who torched Safra. What are you, a ping-pong player?'

'Not since Nixon left China. So who is this Sam Mazandaran, and why might I miss him?'

'He's a player, but the game's not table-tennis. And I have no idea why someone like you would be going to see someone like him; GL didn't say, and I assumed you'd know. Actually I doubt that you don't: you're just fooling with me because you think I'm an insignificant cog in the works. I won't bother to warn you that could be an error.'

'Another spoke might get broken?'

'Yeah. And somebody's wheel fall off.'

'Not yours, I trust.'

'Flattery's not going to work on me either, guy; or that jumped-up English irony. I don't like the look of you. I'm only relaying what I've been asked to.'

'The look of me just now isn't my fault; and that's not an existential observation. As for what you're relaying, I don't follow. I thought I was being given a lift to find this autistic boy's twin.'

'Maybe you are. Maybe that's how Mazandaran figures. You didn't know the first was with GL, huh?'

'I had only one name – Loretta's.'

'Now you have two. But on this condition – and this is what GL really wants me to say – he's busy down there or he would himself. He does it as a favour: he's a generous guy. But on no condition are you to let them know where you come from, how you got his name, who drove you, any of it. Gianni Liskau's not in this. Get it?'

I was on the point of answering *nyet*, but you could see from the straight line of her features that honesty was only superficially the best policy with the type. How our world changes! Emily Dickinson becomes a hard guy while the Italian *capo* who's her apparent boss appears as a genial *philosophe*, even apostle of Love.

I shrugged. She could take that as concessive or not as she wished. In the event, she simpered, then removed her sharp shanks from my presence, leaving me again to the still and susurrus of those natural elements, in which I bathed. Forgive the phrase, Dad, but that's how it felt. I slipped back to drifting, just rocking in that cradle of the historical world's oldest *mare;* and you know what? I was prepared in the moment just to *enjoy*, as they say: just to loll in the present, to *be*. So what if I had a purpose? Did I, after all? If so, what was it? I'd come here for Alexandra, half sleepwalking. I'd stepped up a plank on an invitation, and now? I was drifting, just drifting, an idea of Loretta at the wheel. The actress's face intruded, superimposed on the lippy one of the pair who had burned. Did the factotum share a feature or two with the other? Everything blended, as subconscious images will. Jimmy I recognized – he was a version of the young neo-con transformed, and yet... I couldn't locate this shriek, this cry I had heard or was hearing. And it was more like a woman's than a boy's, or young man's; nor a woman in flame so much as in pleasure... Then I was awaking to copper dawn over a corniche. In my state of rocking arousal, I wondered: could it have been a moan of sexual ecstasy?

4.

One of the sleek Lancias sped me along the route of the Gran Prix; now I was lifted to the top of a last, modern tower at the end of Avenue Princesse Grace. It was the second time in one morning I'd been sucked upwards. The first had been when more Lancias met the yacht at Fontvieille and I was whisked to the crest of the Rock where Liskau kept a villa or apartment or whatever you wanted to call that amalgam of splendour and *kitsch*. On its terrace I had lost a precious hour. Pallor had peeled off the face of the Med while whatever I'd wanted for breakfast was served. In a blessed shelter of coastal pine, hydrangea, oleander and bougainvillea in purple and white, I had watched haze disperse and sea return to sapphire under blue. Far below Liskau's yacht had slipped out of the harbour with more crew and on a stronger puff of breeze, antique masts in full sail.

It was beyond the horizon by the time I'd set out for this second upward-sucking. So much for sojourns under two stars at Cannes. Whatever a Lancia driver said to get me into the well-guarded fortress, I was now standing inside the double doors of a penthouse.

Its football field of a living-room spread down and out towards further panoramas of blue over azure. I was alone, it appeared. The lift had arrived direct from the lobby and, apart from a susurrus deep along one side, there was no sign of life here to greet me.

You could study objects – that's what Dad might have done, I reflected. He came to mind because most of the stuff recalled L.A. – gargantuan paintings, Museum of Contemporary Art sort of thing, not quite decipherable abstracts, 'two warts on a fanny', as he would have quipped. I, being posh, couldn't afford such a put-down. But though Liskau's Géricault drawings had appealed to me more, I wasn't entirely hostile to these streaks of black, orange and brown in almost articulate swirls that filled acres of canvas on two endless walls stretching down to a barrier of sliding-glass. The space was a low barn – how else would you fill it? Panels behind paintings, faced in blond wood, were punctuated by Corinthian columns. The ceiling was pale, flesh-coloured you might say, with cream cornices and four *faux* Venetian chandeliers at regular intervals.

A hotchpotch? – I was trying to make up my mind, taking a careful step forward, when the source of the susurrus came into view. It was a young man, much younger than you'd expect in that plutocrat's den. He hadn't been visible or very audible at first. The chair he sat in, an ersatz version of an 18th century wingback, huge rattan thing (it was all rattan here) with honeydew cushions, had enclosed him; nor was he big. It was only a second before he stood, but in that glimpse, as he listened to his cell-phone, he looked like a ten-year-old far away in a daydream of toy soldiers, model cars or whatever boys of that age obsess on. Being decades removed from it myself, I was at a loss as to what might be traversing his psyche.

He snapped the phone shut.

I said: 'They told me to come up. I was expected.'

'By who?'

The voice sounded like an oboe. But it hadn't said *whom*.

'Mr Mazandaran, I guess.'

The boy – he couldn't have been over twenty – managed to seem eager and dismissive at the same time. 'He's not here.'

'I was told that this was his apartment.'

'May be. But he's gone.'

For twenty, he had snap – a kid with chutzpah. So was this Raphael? He didn't look like his twin – a bit more like his mom.

'I see a boy in an apartment that doesn't belong to him but who acts like he's in charge.' – This brought on something resembling a smile, the assumption of power seeming to please him. 'Do you work for Mazandaran, or –'

'Why are you here?'

It wasn't a threat, or didn't sound like one. It even seemed to hold a hint of familiarity, though if I'd met him before I couldn't locate it.

'Have you seen me somewhere?' I asked.

'I don't recognize your face.'

I gave him the benefit of doubt – i.e., a pause to take in my crooked features. In the mutual size-up, I noted that one day he might have a paunch, or pigeon breast. This was no more than a sign of pride in posture as yet, nor unbecoming. He was a good-looking kid, though not shockingly so like his brother. The hair, curling slightly, was destined to recede with the years; pale brown on top, it was blond only at the tips. Eyes were the same colour as Jimmy's, though darker, like the sea. They had a faint shape of almonds about them, as if gypsies had been involved in his pre-history.

'Are you Rafe?' I asked.

Familiarity and promise seemed to drain from his features. The brows drew in, articulating a frown.

'Why are you here?' he repeated, and it did sound like some sort of a threat this time.

I stated my name and told him who'd sent me.

'She doesn't know where I am. Who told you?'

I couldn't explain without violating Liskau's condition. I guess I must have felt something like fealty to him then, because what I came back with was: 'I can't tell you – not yet.'

'Does this have to do with James?'

His attitude, unreadable. That could become an asset in time, but for now you'd expect a kid in his position to ask about his mother, why she had sent me, whether she was happy, safe – all the things you're supposed to want to know about the vessel that's brought you into this world and nurtured you with its blood. But here was *l'étranger* in the making. Or was it?

'It may,' I nodded, realizing vaguely that the situation of his twin might hold some clue, or at least his attention. 'We can talk about that. First I have something to tell you about Alexandra.'

I used her name to underline the closeness between us and disarm something Oedipal in him, or possibly just petulant. 'I don't want to know,' is what he answered; and though it didn't sound spiteful, when he added 'I don't want her butting in on my life', a sense of strangeness slipped around, as if some ghostly presence had stepped in the door. Was a cloud closing over the seascape out there? Light seemed to fade at the far end of the room, an ambient darkness to enfold it. Did I hear voices? 'What's going on?' 'Who is he?' Dizziness surged, recalling the night of the fire. It seemed to go hot, even blazing around me. Voices cried – French, Arabic; then came a shriek. Shadows of silhouettes merged into red, and I was gone.

'Just don't think,' a voice muttered, 'that because I got you out of there, it's going to end up at the Oscars.'

It seemed like days later. Where I had been and why I was again in the back of one of Signor Liskau's grey Lancias was a riddle.

'I told them,' the actress went on, 'that you were one of mine.'

It was night now. We were cruising.

'Told who? And one of your what?'

She looked at me crossly, as much as you could say in that half-light. The face made you wonder: how could she rate as one of the top sex symbols in our world? But that would have involved discussion about who does the ratings – not a topic I was about to take up with my head throbbing like a tumescent member.

'Not lovers, anyhow.'

'I should be so lucky.'

'No you shouldn't.' – She looked away, as if in self-deprecation. 'The police didn't rough you up, I hope.'

I had an idea of an office, of uniforms coming in, of a map with threads on it, of a balding young man in a photo against red-and-white-checks. 'That's where I've been?'

'Don't pretend you didn't know.'

I tried to piece it together. 'I must've been sapped; injected with something. That's how it feels.'

'They picked you up from the bouncers at the Billionaires. Maybe they worked you over.'

'Billionaires?'

'Nightclub, east side of town. I was in there too. Seemed pretty weird. I was on my way out when you were being shovelled into the back of a Monagasque cop car. I'd been there an hour: why hadn't I seen you? Something was fishy. So I followed.'

'Who? The cops?'

'O for fuck's sake, the bouncers weren't going anywhere.'

My head was truly engorged. Dizzy, grizzling, parched... Could I put it together? 'So then?' I asked.

'So I went in, after a while. Had to think about it – in my position you have to take care. On the other hand, Monaco doesn't like scandal. So I took the odds.'

I pondered, and got nowhere. 'Odds on what?'

'I guess you *are* banged up, or my instincts are crap. I thought you were half a smart guy; maybe you're just another chump. Whatever, I got you out.'

'What, bailed me?'

'Not exactly. People like me don't have to do that – let's not go into it. I've done enough to atone for my sins for one day. Where do you want to be dropped?'

Without knowing where I'd been, it was hard to say where I was going. Something was haunting – the face of that boy. Where was *he* now? What had happened?

As if tracking a parallel thought, she said: 'They're in Italy next.'

To which I naturally asked, 'Who?'

'Joe Liskau, who else? The boat. I got off.'

A cry of pleasure, or was it of pain, came back. Or was it just my poor head throbbing?

'You OK?' she wondered, almost with concern.

'I'll manage,' I managed, but I thought: would I?

'Let the driver take you home,' she suggested. 'Can you remember where that is?'

I looked at him – no, couldn't trust it. 'Actually I can't,' I answered, which was not far from true.

'Oh brother!' – A pregnant pause. 'Well, I guess that means you'll have to come with me.'

This thought turned us to stone. The car whirred on somewhere. All of a sudden she turned and whispered, 'Kiss me.'

'Wha'?'

'O for fuck's sake!' – And she took my banged skull between her palms and suctioned my mouth onto hers.

I was too stupefied to feel much, even with this immortal. She knew it but, being professional, gave the driver a juicy rearview before unlipping me. 'Over there, under the *porte-cochère*,' she said to him and, popping a door – 'If you tell a soul what I picked up, I'll have you fired.' To this he smirked, as did the liveried guy who ushered us into a lift. 'Bye,' she called back, blowing froth off our tonguing, and, as the lift doors closed – 'You too, big boy.'

So I was sucked up for the third time in – well, you tell me how many days it was. Something clicked then. I had a distant image of Dad with Mom in a scene out of some old *noir*, and when doors opened onto a dim lobby, I tried to resume what had gone on below.

'Not on your life, pal.' – She straight-armed me off. 'That was for Joe's benefit. Nothing to do with you.'

'I thought you told the driver – '

'To tell no one. Best way of making sure he gets the word. And since he's at sea and it's two in the morning, that means tomorrow, or later this a.m. – whatever. You've got, say, six hours; eight maybe. So think. Talk. Help me here. What the fuck's going on?'

I stared at her. 'I thought you could tell me.'

'Me? What do I know? I'm just an air-headed half-Kiwi. Don't you read hairdressers' magazines?'

She flipped on a switch. God! it was bright.

'Sorry!' she giggled – girls just want to have fun. 'You need an Advil maybe? Lie down, over there.'

Twisting a dimmer, she made the savage blaze die, and I went for the sofa indicated. (You could've dropped on three before reaching it.) She meanwhile dove into another barn of a room and shortly had it pulsing at multiplex levels with the waltz out of *La Traviata*. Revolving around, she communed with a phantom: Garbo after her tryst with John Barrymore in *Grand Hotel*. Or was she just playing the Parisian courtesan mooning over her underage lover? Whatever, it took a heartbeat to suss that it was not *Gioia* she was feeling as she lip-synced, but something akin to need for a primal scream.

'You have neighbours?' I asked as bombast died.

'Honey, this is the tax-haven. See those pillars of glass over there? Empty. Notice the missing lights?'

Music again. A reprise of *Sempre libera*. So was that the issue here? too much freedom? Was it the same story as Dad had experienced back in Mom's posh divorceé's salon? And what had been his take on it? He had never said, not in so many words; nor had he tried to arrest it, so far as I knew, only to clean up one or two consequences of it. So what about me? What should *I* be doing, entering my own version of

34

it? just drift into the swirling? look for some spar to grab onto? a shore to pull myself up on? 'You do have a purpose in being here, don't you?' somebody had said. Not her. She was into the eddies herself, whirling exuberantly, yet even more unwillingly than I. That much was clear by the time, Callas having repeated herself twice, she cut the sound, threw herself onto a twin sofa and asked me, 'So?'

'So?'

'So who are you?'

It occurred to me even before she'd half-explained that Liskau had told her *niente*. I was just some guy who'd been on the boat at Cannes when they'd showed and stepped off, as she had, at Fontvieille. Why I had done so? that boy's face was still haunting. But her?

'No one,' I shrugged. 'Or whoever you want me to be… Mind if I ask you one?'

'You show me yours and I'll let you see mine?' – She chuckled as if naughty, though dreamy and tired; at which point I realized she was probably well-loaded too.

'OK, mine's this. Why did *you* get off here?'

That sobered her up, anyhow to the extent that she stumbled erect and demanded, 'Wanna drink?' – She poured vodka.

I said: 'Seemed like you had a thing going on that boat.'

'"A thing going"?' Bottle in hand, she revolved the moon face. 'What do you mean, mate?' – It was savage, defensive. 'You know nothing – *no thing at all*. If you did, I might snuff you myself. Or…' Here it got juicy, because she burst into tears. 'Omigod!'

'What?'

'Oh! Oh no, nothing. Everything. I forgot something… I need insurance; protection… I got *you* out of shtuck. Can't you help *me*?'

The speed of this *volte-face* was impressive. Was she not drunk after all? Was Garbo the right referent: actress on a roll? Or *was* she Mom, playing the big scene with the hard-to-get gumshoe in a bedroom atop a Hollywood hill? – Whatever. There she was on my sofa and breathing into my ear again, 'Kiss me, now!'

So I did. And she wept. Broke down, you might say, right there in my arms. Heaved and moaned to such a degree that it went far beyond acting or drink, or seemed to. It bore down on you like a wail in a nightmare, a scream in the psyche, some cry for God or humanity. So I rocked her – what else could you do? So she got me, or should I say we got each other? The fact is that, as dawn seeped its way through a crack in her curtains, I was beside her on a sea of a bed, sheets pulled back to expose what half a world longed to gaze at via big screen, mobile image or computer download. But recalling what she'd said about Liskau in the a.m. and realizing I was in shtuck or might be, I got up and, dressing, sloped off from that pretty position without adieu.

5.

The Billionaire's? No, couldn't go there. Monaco police? That didn't seem wise either, under the circs. I hadn't finished my job here – talking with Rafe – let alone tied up the loose ends fluttering around it like tassels on a charity-ball hostess's gown. Alexandra? I couldn't turn up there without answers – not and approve of myself or please an all-too-present ghost of Dad. So I drank my espresso, put a coin on a counter and hopped the first train back to Cannes.

It was near empty. Commuters all came from the other direction, Monaco being the City of the Côte. I thought about the Tube and what a contrast this made to it. They were wedged in in the cars here flying east, but the view out the windows was no black tunnel with false light at the end. It was heaven *tout court* – pearl-blue, green, puce, white over ochre, sienna, gold of sand, lace of foam. Out there transcendence, eternity; on the other side, paternal drama of corniche; on both, pink and tan conurbations crowned with hotels and villas of the *bel époque*… So it was seedy, imperfect, even malign. But that could have its attractions too, couldn't it?

Evading the peep shows across from Cannes station, I dove into the square where market day set up. Fish stalls, cheese vans, all manner of fruit n' veg as well as t-shirts and flip-flops, candies and toys, garden pots, plants and whatever brought in by small traders from Draguignan, Aix… At a far corner in a bar where locals gathered, I had a second espresso et croissant, then made my way down the few blocks to where Dad might have gone for a reading.

The Old Timer belonged to the same homily-and-grit generation.

Picture Walter Huston in *The Treasure of the Sierra Madre,* and you pretty much have it. 'I'm post-*Casablanca*,' was his riff; 'one of the guys stayed after the War, never went back. There's one up in Paris over ninety now. I'm a youngster – only eighty-three.'

I did my maths and placed him with Dad's little brother, the runt of the litter as Mom used unkindly to say. He was the same height, bent in half to duck into his cabin.

'Cup a tea?' he said, fussing with a pot over which a Beatnik might have incanted *OM*. 'What is it exactly you need help with?'

'Loretta Boyar. You directed me to her.'

'When?' he grumped, dishing gunpowder out of a tin.

'Afternoon, two / three days ago. Remember?'

'Maybe yes, maybe no. Lots of fellers come by here all the time; an' since I'm too old or lazy to take 'er out, I sit on deck like on my front stoop an' say howdy to most.'

I'd felt special, he could see; so he was bumping me down. Old cusses fond of luring you in, only to shove you away...

'Well, whether you remember or not – '

'I remember, goddammit. Burnt face, bandage... How'd it happen? Make a mistake lightin' a reefer?'

I sniggered. He raised a shade of a grin.

'OK, Loretta... Like a daughter to me. Has been ever since she was knee-high to a 'hopper skittering down that quai. So let's get this straight: mess her around and I'll even up that unburnt half of yours.' – He brandished the kettle.

'Don't waste your hot water, pop. I like being a magpie. And I'm partial to her too, but not in a way that should rile you.'

'What, ain't fast enough for you?'

That got to me, given the previous night. 'Cut me some slack, man. I've only met her once.'

'Well, if you like her, why not try again?'

On this circular note, we sat down to tea. It was strong as boiled root and as sweet as molasses from the sugar he dumped in it, without asking if I wanted any. Still, I drank up like a man and prepared for a stroke. While waiting for it, I put to him,

'Why's she working for Liskau?'

He fixed me with alert, north of Michigan eyes. 'Why not? She's a skipper; he's got a boat.'

'How long has she had that job?'

'What are you? IRS? CIA?'

Sighing, I thought about invoking Dad. Several paperbacks about him decorated a shelf behind the built-ins we sat on. But not wanting to torpedo my credibility so quickly, I told him about Alexandra instead – the fire and my 'mission' to find her boys.

'Who are you? Prince Valiant?'

I coloured, though arguably that was the tea. 'Couldn't I be a guy who just wants some facts? Three people – no, four – are dead, and my movie-star mug'll never be the same.'

'Forget it. Gals prefer rough.'

That spoke a slim volume about his fifty-odd years in Cannes harbour. Loretta – *was* she his daughter?

'What did the flics say?' he went on.

'Arson. Land development scam.'

'Up there? Maybe. What else?'

'Nothing I know of.'

'They question you?'

'Briefly.'

'Anyone other?'

'Lebanese woman, high flyer; gave her the works. Some North African staff too.'

'I see.'

'You see what?'

His shrewd blues scanned the horizon: steel in mixed sun after a spat of night rain. 'French authorities know what they're up to. In my time I've watched how they watch, when they move, when they don't. Specially with foreigners, they play a close game. Ever wonder why so many filthy rich get off living year-in year-out here without paying tax? Don't kid yourself. They know what's going on and can come down sharp as a guillotine-blade if they need.'

I nodded. 'In this case?'

'How would I know? Maybe their theory has back-up and they're just waiting for the next shoe to drop. Why not go ask Joe Liskau?'

He said this without any evident game-playing. It seemed to get somewhere, if not very far. Knowing he was unlikely to give me more in one visit, I stood. 'Thanks for the tea, pop.'

'Any time. Drop by again if you're in the area.'

'I may just.'

I stepped out and up. He followed and from that bent-over posture scanned what had been a floating home for him for half a life.

'She's a good 'un,' he sighed. 'Too much for an old man, though; can't keep 'er in trim. You ain't in the market, are you?'

I twisted my face into the best facsimile of a grin it could muster. 'You never know.'

'That's right. An' some a you guys never will.'

That could piss you off. Was he ventriloquizing for Dad? – I had to get smart now, in somebody's word. I had shake off the victimhood of a messed-up face and whatever it seemed to justify in drift. I had to be what Alexandra thought or wished me to be – a 'hero', or at least shadow of Dad. But how exactly? and for whom?

Circumambulating, I watched mid-morning light paint the harbour in colours of un-besmirched dreams. I passed that far slip where Liskau's yacht had been. Hand it to him, it was a sight sweeter than the hunks of formica the spivs and chancers purchased on ill-gotten gains banked in Cayman or Guernsey. So was that why Loretta worked for him? hard to imagine *her* on one of those floating jacuzzis. She was a sailor down to the calluses, you could see. Even the Timer was a port-hugger by contrast, living too much by the eye and ear to be wholly a creature of currents and breeze.

The smell of the place made you long to be out there, beyond where diesel perfumed it. The clang of the cables, gentle on a rising south-westerly, recalled some past life where sensations like these swept civilization away, leaving you as spellbound as an autistic boy… Loretta doted on him, I mused, the face reappearing. Jimmy wasn't a protégé to her so much as an emanation of longing – that's how I read it. But… 'You're too romantic,' Mom used to say; 'not enough in *real* world – the fault of your dad.'

That could piss you off too. At the same time, it brought back the Alpes-Maritimes as they'd looked from the train passing through Antibes earlier. There'd been an icing on them, night's rain having turned to frost higher up. It would be gone by the time I'd finished my third croissant et café on the Croisette, but not before they'd evoked the mountains ringing L.A. and Palm Springs on clear December mornings when I'd been young.

Dad had loved that sight, Mom used to say. She did too, I mused and recalled how I'd assumed it was what brought them together. But shared aesthetics are rarely enough, are they? Attractions born out of blazes can hardly to live up to the splendour that triggered them; dull greys and long winter days of Reality mean certain doom. What had happened to them, I found myself wondering as I had many times, and downed a second cognac to chase heartburn.

Blame these sentiments on it. Softly, they died as I made my way up to my flea-bag, which was still there, as was the Arab at the desk. He looked me up without question as to where I'd been for two nights. Curiously, he grinned – whiff of her perfume? Whatever, the key was in my hand and I up to my safe place to doze and prepare for what it was now clear I had to…

An hour later and I was shaved, douched and down in the street getting a haircut and stuff to put over my face to make it seem less egregious. Strolling into a men's shop, I bought the latest in sharp jeans, a Lacoste-type shirt – not one of GL's – and light cashmere pullie to drape over the neck. Some chic brand of sunglasses, Gucci loafers *sans* socks, belt with designer logo on buckle, and I was set. No one would notice me making a stakeout. I was like every Swiss Bank account wannabe on the Côte.

Checking my C2 out of Place Lamy, I cruised up to the Péage and turned east. The car didn't flatter the image; on the other hand, I wasn't prepared to spread an incomplete pack of credentials across a counter – two sets of cops had a line on me now. So I sped on past Nice Airport without trading up for a Merc. The Citroën could be trashed in the inevitable car-chase – I had full insurance: I was that kind of guy.

Winding events back, I flicked brains on power. The actress – she'd saved me, roped me into her bed: what was in that? Nothing probably. Spur of the moment. Only a bounder or blackmailer could have played it for more, and a blind drunk could see I was neither. Billionaire's? Why had she been there? Again little in it or, if there was, nothing I could see. Why *I* had been there was another question: the first I needed an answer for. Between being sapped at the end of the principality and turfed into a cop car by bouncers lay ten unknown hours. On the far side of them stood Alexandra's other twin boy.

He loomed up again, asking some kind of question. Had he actually put one? I couldn't say now – memory opaque. I had an impression – everything was an impression in this light-dappled place – that there had been more than a simple 'Who are you?', 'What are you doing here?'; but if so, what? Now there were also my questions in return: where are *you*? are you OK? is there some kind of trouble out there? do you need help? – The ghostly presence seemed to say *Yes* and *No* at the same time, which I guess added up to *Maybe*.

This wasn't satisfactory, but it was more than the Timer had offered. Two further remarks made it surer: his mom's that he could answer 'if he feels like it' and Liskau's that he could explain to his autistic brother 'if he should wish'. The boy was key, yes. And there was one more thing: I wanted to see his face again. There was something familiar in it I couldn't place. Did his mom know? Wasn't that why she had drawn me into this blind odyssey to begin with?

I didn't consult any handbook or those pulps about Dad: detection, like spying, must be nine-tenths a bore. I sat in a café in San Roman for hours – *Nice Matin*, a demi, *Herald Trib*, more café. Cars sped by, not many – Avenue Princesse Grace, end of the place; Lavrotto, a last outpost. I clocked the usual BMWs and Mercs slipping out of the garage under the tower; now and then came an Aston or Bentley, Maserati Quattroporte, not much – only enough to support the populace of a mid-sized African township for a year.

The tax haven! Well, this wasn't about politics so far as I knew, and I had my own stash of safe mutual funds; so let's not be hypocrites. Dad might have been non-plussed, his pal Noorgaard too, along with the old guy in Cannes harbour but… It was a wait. There was stuff in the *Trib* to distract me – Iraq, inflation, poor Lebanon. I parsed the back-stories and dug into subtexts, had a *pression*, a ham sandwich, a glimpse of a garish opera-star behind one wheel, a London mogul who'd got rich ripping off GL tops at another. Two Albanian tarts passed on the arm of a high-roller from Baku; it rained as rain only in beauty spots can – hard as a vixen's wee-hours rant. Then, just as she was exhausting herself into dribs, five late-model, moon-blue Alfas smoothed up out from under, each aquiline and alert in front and peremptorily proud at the tail. Pay dirt! just what I'd been hoping for – this guy Mazandaran's troop.

Was the boy with them? Nine-tenths waiting... They swung off west. I hopped into my C2, humped Monte down into La Condamine – the poor, by Monagasque standards, part of town – and caught up with them crouching like panthers at the light by the tunnel that bore through the Rock. Making green as they popped clutches, I realized they'd be in no rush till we got past the pay-booths. Settling two cars behind, I hung in there. Emerging into a blessed, sea-gilt evening light, I had to keep rpm's up to six grand to match their five; but Alfas are built for handling, not speed, so I didn't fall too far back. Beauty passed in the long crépescule. How different it must seem behind windshields at 160 kph than in Napoleon's travelling-coach – one more reason to be at sea, I noted: contrast in style between Liskau and Mazandaran. This was premature, of course. I knew no more about the latter than the look of an apartment, choice of staff cars and a bump on the head. That and the drugging, if drugging it was, could have had nothing to do with him. More likely it had everything.

Exit for Alexandra's hurtling past, orange gave way to purpling blues, and before black had taken over the heavens completely, the convoy reached Le Muy and turn for St Trop. Obvious really. If I lost them now, I'd find them with a question or two at Café des Boules or du Port. St Tropez I had known since an era when her posh crowd had worn feathered earrings and fancied itself chic because someone had at one time snorted a line with somebody who'd shared a bed with Mick Jagger. Halcyon days. Now this stretch of coast was like Irvine enclosing Laguna. Still there was charm here, up in the old town. But that's not where the Alfas were heading.

They swung around Ste Maxime, lights rippling the Golfe. Port Grimaud rose: it hadn't existed when I'd first come. A sequence of new roundabouts led to quaint suburbs – Cogolin, La Croix Valmer, gathering metropolis. One Alfa swung off on a spoke for La Foux; others continued more or less straight for the port before veering away short of it. They carried on towards Ramatuelle through the foothills, land virgin for the most part, planted in grapes. Now and then up popped a warehouse for fertilizer, agri-machinery; then we were into a new roundabout and off to a new shopping-centre, small, not yet set up, designed to offend the environs somewhat less than the Casino Géant and big sheds sprouting behind, tugging Toulon to the east. The Alfas turned in a lot and purred to a stop in front of a large, indistinct block set in a grove of cork oak. I kept my wits about me and carried on as if kms of tarmac lay between C2 and supper in Le Lavandou.

Such a smart guy. This private dick gig, what a doddle? – Such a prat! It hardly occurred to me before it was too late that I was, in Dad's phrase, as obvious as a fat lady at a firemen's ball. By the time I'd turned back and coasted to the far side of the unfinished centre, slipped out of my Citroën and started towards the building, a friend or two was waiting for me.

'Looking for something, hombre?'

The accent wasn't French, and there was no angle in *pretending* to be Mexican. 'Comment?' I said.

A shadow moved from between potted palms placed in front of a long, low, grey structure. I saw no one else but could feel a presence behind. Why fight it, I thought and in a sudden, unrehearsed gesture put my arms up. Sure enough, hands slipped around my chest and started to tap down.

'Just like airline check-in, pal,' came the Tijuana twang. 'Lots of terrorists nowdays. Can't be too sure.'

He stepped into the light, such as it was – a mild glow from around a word in raised capitals beside copper-bronze doors: P-R-O-I-E.

'Mind telling us what you're after?'

He had a pig-tail somewhat longer than Liskau's but appeared decades younger, taller, heavier-set. The one at my back came into full view. Both wore blue-black, like the Alfas: t-shirts, leather jeans.

'If you prefer to speak English,' I offered, putting on a Midi accent, 'I might ask you.'

'I see. The McDonald's bomber, huh?'

'Comment?'

'Cut the comedy, jack. You're no more French than I'm from Oran. If you're curious, say. In fact, why not come in? Mr Mazandaran might be willing to interrupt his meeting to explain a few facts.'

It wasn't the sort of invitation you refused. But they had to resist the strong-arm follow-through. As we stood on the verge of our dance as it were, two more cars pulled up: a Porsche and, I think, Audi TT. Out stepped two or three Parisian types, lightly-clad, one toting a folder, possibly architect's plans. Another quipped 'Bon soirée' with an irony lost on my Southern Cal minders; but it was enough to keep them from beating the merde out of me. They pulled open the heavy doors and passed through. We followed.

6.

In a room like a bunker Mazandaran sat. Thirty-odd, swart-skinned, thick-browed, chimp-lipped, he sported a tuft between mouth and chin but no moustache or goatee. A high-necked, midnight-blue *blouson* unbuttoned to sternum was muscled in by a waistcoat in luminous shark. The rest of him, visible only in slashes under a glass table-top, comprised for the most part two elongated trainers set daintily on a Persian carpet. Neo-Bauhaus chairs were scattered around, two or three occupied by heavies dressed not unlike the hombré and friend who'd frog-marched me in. Others were just being taken by the Frenchmen, when the big guy said,

'Hey Philippe! Barzan, 'fore we get to it… why not go check out what we've been doing? San's in there with the tech guys; cast a cold eye, let me know where we've fucked up.'

The voice was lighter than its owner's aura, a whine underneath. Despite that, it carried enough authority to clear the room of all but gang members, leaving him staring at, or apparently through, me.

'José, you guys get those pizzas, or is this half-burnt piece of meat all we're havin' for supper?'

'In the car, Sam. Thought snoopers might be a priority.'

'Good thinkin'. You two go get 'em; feed the others. I gotta work up an appetite.'

It was like that. Hard-guy stuff Dad would have been at home in. Me? I might have fouled my shorts if his lip hadn't curled into a smirk from the schoolyard. Hombrés dispatched, he seemed to be trying to decide what record to play next – CD to his generation. I pretended to study a wall on which spread a map of the coast with pins in it.

'We know who you are,' he said once no more than two heavies were left. – The lighting was mild, the décor pale grey. It was not comfortless here, only nerve-jangling.

'That's nice,' I gave back in a sound like a gargle.

'Yeah, nice. What we don't know is how you got into my apartment the other day. Care to tell?'

'Not really.'

'I guessed not, but you know what? Where I come from, which is where you half come from, I hear, breaking and entering's a felony.'

'I didn't break. And where the other half of me comes from beating and drugging an intruder's a crime.'

'Yeah? I guess that's why I never had time for that Brit snit shit. A man ain't worth squat unless he does his dirty work for himself.'

'That's a philosophy.'

'Seems like yours. But not the person or persons' who sent you.'

'Person,' I clarified.

'You sure about that?'

'Yeah. And she's English.'

'Oh yeah. San's mom. We'll get to that. In the meantime, what about the other one?'

'What "other one"?'

'Like I asked, man: the guy who got you in there. Security at that place's s'posed to be like the friggin' White House. That's what they told me when I leased it.'

'I guess you were conned.'

He looked to his henchmen. One of them, a blond out of the era of Dewey Weber, rolled peepers. More stuff out of Dad's book.

'Guess I was,' Mazandaran mused, gazing back to me. 'Guess I'm just some dippy ho-dad from Pepperdine, huh?'

I let that float. 'I was asked to find an old friend's son,' is what I said. 'I was asked to tell him her house had been torched, some folks had died and she was shaken. For that I've been smacked, doped, thrown to the cops and now grilled. A guy who knows how it feels to be cheated ought to have sympathy.'

'O I do, man; ask around. I'm a big-hearted dude. And you weren't smacked. It was ether.'

His mobile broke into 'My Boy Lollipop'. Snapping it open, he listened for a beat. A grunt, and he motioned a henchman to run. This one gone, it left only Dewey, grinning crook-faced at me, as only old surfers can. I returned the compliment.

'Girls here yet?' the boss meanwhile growled to the slip of alloy in hand. 'Well soon as they are, get 'em rehearsing. I'm not opening with just a few deadbeats from San Clemente doing the frug.'

'Hey! I'm from San Clemente,' Dewey objected.

Snapping his phone shut, Mazandaran chuckled. 'Timer,' he threw at me as if bygones could be bygones and we were on the same team, 'you grew up in So Cal, they say. Wherebouts? Poodle Springs?'

Dewey laughed. They were back in the saddle.

'I lived in Palm Desert a year and a half,' I said. 'And summer vacations as a boy.'

'Not much, man. Not enough. Ever go to the beach?'

'Topanga. Point Dume. Malibu sometimes.'

'Then you know the score. This ancient gremmie can tell you' – he nodded to his man. 'When a wave's crowded, it's the one who gets in first who has the right of way, huh? But there's an exception. If the guys in the wave are all short stuff hanging onto a rail hoping to stand for two seconds before wiping out and the guy paddling behind has grown up doing Makaha and is known for hanging ten down twelve foot glass tubes, you get out from in front of him, right?'

'Awesome!' crowed the surfer.

I waited. Mazandaran did too. When no reaction came from me, he stood up, all six foot four inches of him.

I hadn't noticed his size until then. The head was too small for the torso – say, one to ten. The jeans hung low in a style of recent beefcakes; they were hitched by a belt wide enough to whip a bull. Its buckle was set with stars that shone like diamonds. Maybe they were.

Where did the dough come from? I made a note to Google him if ever I were so lucky as to get out of there.

'Come onto the floor, man,' he said as if we were old pals. 'You might as well see what's shakin'.'

A piece of wall slid back; he stepped through; I noted a Haephaestus limp. Dewey flicked his crop at me, and I followed them into a cavernous space done up like a film set.

The motif was safari. An artificial tree rose in the centre; from its branches hung cages and ropes – you could see how the 'girls' were going to be put to work when they got there. Around a perimeter stood other trees at regular intervals, like columns in a coliseum; on their branches sat platforms resembling Tarzan's tree-house. These held the best tables – private boxes as if, from which Mrs Francis Macomber could gaze down through her lorgnette on a space consisting of more tables strewn round the big tree. Through them wound rock pathways and streams, as if in the Serengeti. Bars and serving stations hid between hummocks and trunks, also a bandstand and apparatus for light and sound. It was all worked out – a construction of art, if to some eyes vulgar; and seeing me staring at a ceiling of galaxies amid floating clouds, the big man evidently experienced a shade of the pride Satan felt on revealing the heavens to Cain.

Devils scurried around, Alfa boys, Parisian fitters, all directed from the middle by Alexandra's son, clipboard in hand.

'San's beautiful,' Mazandaran nodded. 'He's my eyes 'n ears already. Got a real future.'

'"San"?' I repeated, realizing he meant the boy I knew of as Rafe.

'We call him "San", as in San Rafael – get it? He works too. No booze, drugs, women, fudge-packers – clean as a saint. Guys try to pimp him but he just keeps his eyes on the books. Perfect, man. Tell her to back off.'

'Who says she's coming on?' I asked as his mobile chirruped 'My Boy Lollipop' again. Before he could answer, I'd added, 'I just came to deliver a message.'

'He knows, man.' – Then to the alloy: 'Hey sweetie, where you been? I been wasting away… You did, huh?… With *that* guy? You're

pulling my... Hey, no way... Right as rain, babe: standin' right here...'
And with a scowl that may have hid sentiments worse, he handed the
dingus to me.

He could have played this Hollywood twist any way he wanted.
Or was he more wrong-footed than he let on? I still didn't know 'squat'
about him. Was he giving me rope to hang myself with? Did he want
to learn more about what *I* was up to? If so, the info was unlikely to
come via Dewey, which is who he dragooned to return me to the Rock
as per the lady's demand, or instruction. My job may have been to stay
put, but tact of bone structure suggested it was no option. So I left
Rafe trekking around jungle, designating campsites for gunners after
virtual game. Mazandaran flipped his phone shut, barked an order
and, blessing me with another look – not smile of farewell – sauntered
off in the wake of one of his Parisians to bury himself in chat about
whether lights during rain should go purple or green.

I tried to tell Dewey I had a vehicle to transport myself in; he
sneered happily 'Get it tomorrow – or never, thin man.' I tried to step
into the passenger-seat of his Alfa but he nodded *in back*, crinkling his
nose as if I'd fouled myself on meeting him and José. This was untrue,
nor would I have wanted to spoil the new car smell, which in any case
he soon chased by lighting a reefer. Any notion I had of friendly banter
was banged away by a wail of Dick Dale and the Deltones and other
hits from an era when he'd been surfing the Slides.

We were near contemporaries, it appeared. Might even have been
in the same frat had he bothered with anything so effete as college. So
was that my problem, I wondered as we swooped up to the Péage. If
I had evaded all the *de rigueur* crap Mom had prescribed, might I have
grown up as straight as this crooked arrow and been prepared for the
mean streets of Dad? Often, I'd wished *he*'d been around to tell her
about other modes of education. But would he have? Do the mean-
streets guys ever want to stay down 'n dirty? Wasn't Mazandaran
an example? even Dewey-boy here? After days in the sand and high-
school parking-lot, what beckoned but French designers, late model
Alfas and penthouses in *les paradis fiscaux*?

Arriving at a tower that looked vaguely familiar, I prayed he might
let me out to pad off on my own; but 'Not a chance, pal.' By some

sleight-of-hand he came up with a ticket to an underground lot and in we swooped to park next to a silk-finished Maserati. 'Out,' he grunted, killing the t-spark, snuffing a Beach Boys fantasy. 'That's her chassis,' he said of the Maso. 'Boss bought it for her. Don't ding the paint.'

This was all the prelude I would have to what I was now impelled back into. Following orders still, he bunged me into a lift, which sucked us up to whatever button he'd pressed – I didn't catch it this time anymore than on the prior occasion, but it was high. In the lobby in front of her door he thumbed a buzzer. On cue she opened, and he faded away like mid-afternoon's blown-out shorebreak.

'You shouldn't've done it,' is how she began.

There were a number of things this could have referred to. I waited to hear which one she had in mind.

'Nobody does that,' she clarified. – The lights in her place were on dimmer this time.

'Well?' she demanded. 'Why did you?'

'Why did I what?' – The script left few options.

'"Why did I what?"! What kind of line is that? "Why did I *what*?"! O for fuck's sake!'

So here we were again. 'Mind if I sit?' I asked rhetorically, making for the sofa she'd offered mere hours before.

'Mind if you sit? Of course I mind! I should have you thrown out of here and back into the cop shop where I picked you up! Omigod, what an ingrate.'

'"Ingrate". Good word.'

'"Good word"? What is this, man? Who are you to get snotty with *me*? Do you know who you're dealing with? You have any idea what a person like me has behind her?'

'Guys who favour Italian sport cars?'

She gaped, then recovered.

'He's nothing,' she said, lighting a fag. 'Made two indie films, set up a club in boy-town. It's hardly Paramount.'

'Paramount's hardly paramount these days, from what I hear.'

'"From what you hear"?' – She flopped on the sofa opposite mine. 'What you hear must be pretty limited. Why else would you run out on someone like me?'

I stared. She was almost a study in sorrow, but not quite. 'I didn't "run out",' I said. 'That would've involved running in, which I didn't. Besides you can't tell me that night in black satin wasn't an act.'

'O can't I?'

Taking the scripted puff off her fag, she got up and came over to zip lips. I did and didn't want it; she could tell but made as if she couldn't. It took a nice while. Then, back on her own sofa, she tried a new tack – 'I'm at my wit's end, man. I can't fool you, but can I trust you? That's the question.'

No answer. A faraway look. Chewing the air, she took up the Mary Astor riff, *Maltese Falcon*: 'O I'm so tired – so tired of running, of lying... I had hoped...' Then the tears. 'I have tried – I wanted to be better, but...' So it went. And what it held may have been partly the truth, but with fiction so mixed in that it would have taken all the way to a Las Vegas divorce to unravel.

So was this the sort of act Dad had been caught in? Had some late night scene like it ended in producing *me*? What odd trickery our animal rites of conception involve, what weird moans from the female, what impulsion-repulsion from the male! But... why should I have been thinking along these lines just then? This woman didn't want me – that much was clear. She wanted something, was *up to* something; but I'd been around long enough to know when you're an excuse, an entity to fall back on or to rebound off of rather than settle into the arms of as if in sheer bliss.

Well, we played out the scene – it hardly matters how. Lines were said, postures taken, all *moues* and motions of the serial auditionist. Then around dawn she asked me to drive her to the airport. It was time, she said – 'More than time' – to get back to L.A..

She knew how to make herself plain as a washer-woman from Warsaw to book a seat. First class could protect her; doing the counter thing required an act, but she was not a Big Star for *niente*.

Services rendered earned me the Maso. 'Keep it,' she murmured, as if sentimental. 'Stay in the apartment,' she added, as if the devoted wife who knows that hubby will be off with the nearest doxie in hot pants once her weepy departure is finalized.

'That might be dangerous, don't you think?'

She didn't smile then. 'OK, don't. Do what you want to. It's what I do – when they let me.'

So with one capacious handbag and a scarf over the hair, she decamped. Wouldn't even let me walk her to passport control. 'Just go!' she hurled back as if truly grief-stricken. 'Get out of here!'

So I did. And felt almost sorry for myself, though why was about as clear as a dollop of pale ectoplasm.

7.

I wasn't clear about much then, you might say. And you might be right. But I was clear enough not to stay in the apartment or keep the car of a 20-mill-a-film star being chased by a thug and backed by a smoothie like Liskau.

What did these interrelations add up to? I had no more idea than a conspiracy-theorist maundering over the fate of Diana, or who really blew up those towers in old-time New York. Cruising back to St Tropez, I felt myself float. In the realms of the incomprehensible, I was approaching those swirls where you could almost glimpse above or beyond what seemed to be happening here below. But could I grasp it? Could I escape this lower order of being long enough to hold onto big answers? Did I actually want to?

The Maso hummed as if on a cocktail of stardust and brown sugar. It smelled of new leather and whatever sweet scent she'd worn, making my too, too sullied flesh tingle as if after a schoolgirl in heat. Oh well: old guys dream. And I knew who I was. 'Timer', Mazandaran had called me, which is what I amounted to to him – same as the old guy in Cannes harbour to me. So why would an actress or any dish as attractive as her give up her car and her flat, let alone her body, to a banged-up old magpie like yours truly?

It didn't figure. Nor could I make sense still of why she'd been right there to rescue me from the Monaco cops. What *did* make sense? me having been laid out at The Billionaires as a bad drunk? Mazandaran claimed it was ether and I hadn't been slugged; if so, why had I been off with the fairies for eight/ten hours? What had gone on in that nether-world? Was I meant to believe that the effects of the fire had come back, making me wander in some un-recallable limbo, only to be dished up as meat for bouncers?

What would Dad have made of it? I was in no rush to go back to the Timer and decipher his ventriloquism. What might that sly child Raphael have said, he being the last who'd laid eyes on me before the lights went? *That* might be worth knowing, I mused, humming down from Le Muy to Ste Maxime and around to the Presqu'Île. It elbowed aside questions of what on earth was going on between the actress and Mazandaran, or actress and Liskau, to prompt her to turn to me.

I guessed no one would be at PROIE so early, anyhow none of the Alfa boys who might have cared. I was right too – only sound vans, a caterer and measly Porsche were there, the last from the night before possibly. Slipping the Maso into a space not far off, I hid the key under driver's seat and half hoped no one would steal her before somebody wondered why she was *in situ*. Then I padded off to find my measly Citroën, wracked with regret.

No one had disturbed *her*. Whoever would? She was light, pretty, minor – just the job for a soon-to-be quinquagenarian looking for a quiet life. Well, maybe one day I would get it. But no time soon. As I drove off from the building and unfinished centre, there was a euphonic bang; and once smoke had cleared, the rearview informed me that her pretty Maso – yet oddly, not the Porsche – had been vomited like volcanic ash to the sky.

'When in doubt send a man through the door with a gun'? – I burnt rubber through foothills, recalling Dad's phrase. Was it an admission that he too had got lost in the Incomprehensible? If so, what in my present state would be the equivalent? 'When in doubt, don't stick around'? 'Skeedaddle and add up the improbables later'? – I'm a survivor. It's just what I did.

For Alexandra's I headed. She could add it up for me if anyone could. En route I stopped for a much-needed loo; since it was attached to an internet café, I took that chance to google Mazandaran. Some L.A. rag had a piece on his family and ambitions out there; no mention of what he might have been up to here.

Alexandra for her part claimed not to have heard of him.

'Rafe tells me nothing,' she breathed, calm as a statue on the patio where I'd left her. 'I wasn't aware he was on the Continent still, let alone here in France.'

My use to her appeared to be lost in the landscape.

'Sorry, darling,' she sighed, dark glasses fixed to blond fields. 'I've really put you through it, haven't I?'

'You might've told me more before I set off.'

'I might have. I should have. Forgive me. I've been wretched.'

Peering into the maw of her half-ruin, I saw little changed – a few shards of charcoal removed.

'Perhaps Zabiha knows something,' she added.

'Zabiha?' – Years seemed to have passed since that holocaust. 'What would *she* know?'

'About this person Rafe has attached himself to?'

'Mazandaran? Why?'

'Persian Jews. The mid-East…'

'But she's Lebanese. And he was no more than three or four when his family went to the States.'

'Yes, fall of the Shah. It was about then, I should guess, that we became acquainted with her.'

I waited. She made no further connection. I didn't pursue it. She *did* seem wretched. Post-meridian sun caught the lines in her face, turning it into a relief map. She'd taken on years in the days since the fire; had its significance only just hit her? Despair lurked, and I was no help – not even able to offer a good word on her boys. I did my best: said they looked well, seemed productive, happy even. She listened abstractly and, when I'd finished, asked of Jimmy – or James –

'Has Loretta stayed close?'

'So far as I know.'

'It was my main condition. Giovanni can be an angel, but demons have been known to emerge.'

I didn't pursue this either.

'Loretta, thank God, is not one of them,' she added, lighting a flare in my mind of the lynx-woman and porn-lipped one who had gone up in flame.

Was she thinking of them? What *was* she thinking? How much did she know that she wasn't letting on, as glasses drifted back to a middle distance? Why, for instance, had she sent me to Loretta when it was Liskau she'd put in charge of her autistic boy? Why hadn't she said that she'd known *him* for years, decades even, before the London scene she'd flourished in when I'd met her? Was there a story behind it? Had she feared her late husband or his grand friends might be put off by a pre-history involving – well, what? Who? What had Liskau been then that he wasn't now? How did this Alexandra connect with one of, say,

1965? How had she made the transition from model to *grande dame*? Did it matter? Was it my business? What *was* my business now? I'd located her sons, which is all she'd asked for. So was that it? Had I any purpose here anymore? – Only if my name were involved, or the flics cared to link me with a car being blown.

'You've told no one?' she wondered.

'No one about what?'

'Really, any of this.'

'Who would I tell? And why?'

'That's good. I'd like it to stay between us. The police have ideas; they may know more than we do.'

A hand stretched out to a plastic-topped table and fussed with a mess of pink paper I recognized as the weekend *FT*. Folding a page over, she handed me an article detailing development plans for an unspecified area in the Var – more or less where we were sitting. Ambition oozed from it: there would be villas, condos, a golf course, timeshare setups, offshore financing to evade French tax and inheritance laws… It made discouraging reading. Forest and vineyard, the odd farmhouse and maybe even château would have to go. Nothing was said about the planning fights this might entail, nor who had cooked up the scheme – a spokesman, something Ltd, Sp.A or Gesellschaft. Orange County in Provence is what it evoked: gridlock and smog billowing in like a cloudbank from Marseilles.

'So: that's what's behind the fire?'

'So they imagine, or speculate. And who am I to argue? just one of the *anglaises riches* who comes down here year after year to entertain friends that joke about "frogs" and eat at the tables of locals without deigning to speak a word of their language.'

Edward and Luther materialized then. Was she implying that *they* were to blame? Did it suggest another possibility – some local version of the McDonalds' bomber?

We kissed air and I left, with no further remit. Patting my scorched cheek, she led me to the car, remarking that she'd be back in Holland Park before my replacement passport came. Turning in her drive, I weighed up her words, 'The builders say three months, so perhaps by the end of summer…' They tailed into non-conviction, and I drove away wondering: was this all part of some further act? Did she want melancholy to trail me to keep me on scent?

If so, it was hardly necessary. I was on scent anyhow: curiosity, Dad and annoyance guaranteed it; also concern for her boys. I *was* her sole link to them still, I reflected, spitting up stones. But did she want contact with them truly? I had been a young man once: I'd had a mother… and clouds *were* swirling in via Marseilles. Did she just want my assurance they were safe so she could wash her hands of them fully?

At the Péage I turned east. Time had come find where my passport status had got to. Putting my foot on it, I was almost to Mougins before I noticed a moon-blue Alfa behind me. So was this to be the *de rigueur* car chase at last? If so, I had lost before I'd begun. But what to do? let yourself be worked over by an ex-surfer and Chicano from Downey? – Yanqui go home, I chuckled to Dad over my shoulder. But that hardly stopped the Alfa from doing its worst.

It swept down on me like a hawk on a hare in a field. Do prey have some weird sensation of bliss at the instant when destiny strikes? Is there a flare of brilliance before the pain and dead fall? a flash in which the Great Plan becomes clear? or is it all just panic, panting, a vain dash for cover and desperate thrashing of hind legs in blue air?

My version of this was a gavotte of lane-changes and juxtapositions without copula. Between zipping Fiats and bumptious Renaults, the Alfa cruised, making me guess that the driver was José not Dewey, or some thug with a knack for the tango. I jitter-bugged off and watusi-ed around, but the Latin skills of my partner were deft. I had to submit and let his aquiline form rumba me into a lay-by.

Getting out, I raised arms. But here came a shock: no one emerged – no Chicano to frisk me. No one seemed to be in there, which made you half-wonder if the car had been on remote, like some battery toy kids plays with; and for a flash I imagined Mazandaran up a scarp of Esterel giggling over a plastic control-panel. But then someone *was* there. Yes, a palm beckoned over the wheel – what attached?

All was obscure behind mystifications of smoked windscreen and designer lenses. As I approached, the passenger-door popped and I peered in to see the palm beckon again. There was a kind of cool breeze to it in the midst of the glare and roar of the autoroute. This harmonized with a crooning that emerged, retro style, in a language indistinct but later to be identified as Occitan. The shades sloped towards a crew-cut. I hadn't seen this one before, I thought as he murmured 'Vite!' What about little Citroën I was about to object but, as if reading my mind, he added, 'Oubliez tout cela.'

Well, you make a decision, or Fate makes it for you. Maybe it was to do with the music or some fascination born out of not knowing the other side – Provence west of St Tropez; Toulon, a *vrai* Midi. Not that I knew this guy was from there. But in the brief flash of impressions that crowd in on you he seemed authentic enough, whatever the circumstances. So I took a seat.

The door shut; central locking clicked; we were off and, apart from 'Merde!' under the breath five seconds later, he uttered no more. The *merde* was in response to what flared in his rearview – obligingly, he cocked it so I could see. A column of black whooshed into azure, scats of red-orange in it. *Oubliez tout cela* indeed. I could forget about what to say to the flics or rent-a-car folks. Little Citroën was yet further removed than an actress's Maso to vehicular heaven.

Occitan crooned – something about 'ma polida'. The driver lit a Gauloise, offering me one. I don't smoke anymore, but I accepted, just for auld lang syne. Poor Citroën, I thought for an idiot's second – shock, doubtless. Then a fug of black tobacco and what seemed like Delta blues mixed with Piaf absorbed me; and I waited to be delivered to whatever new initiation attended.

Absurdly, I found myself wondering if Mazandaran and Co had eaten their pizza. This was a moon-blue Alfa, right? fleet of his mob, though Land Rovers or gross Hummers might have been more apt. What did that tell you? Nothing I could put a finger on. Nonetheless I was free to tremble for twenty minutes about car bombs, hard guys, conspiracy theory and what-not... mafiosi, contract ops laid off from the KGB, IRA, alphabet soup.

But we were not bound for the L.A. crowd's door, nor was I to be worked over by hombrés and surfers. The driver pulled off not far beyond Nice airport and made for the old town. He found a café and ordered a pastis, offering me one in the same taciturn gesture he used to tip a Gauloise from a pack. In for a penny in for a pound. I was louchely preparing to throw back a maiden sip when, spotting a Rossini-grey Lancia out the window, he drained his glass, grabbed his key off the zinc-top and deserted me, grinning back 'Ciao.'

T-spark, Alfa hum... then in front of his empty stood a new driver. This one I recognized: he was the same who had got me into the penthouse at the far end of Ave Princesse Grace. A friendly *je ne sais quoi* in the eye caught my raised glass and inquired 'Une autre?' Would booze have helped? Dad might have thought so; likewise M. Maigret. But I declined. So after he'd tossed back a *noisette* and laid down three coins down for the pleasure, I found myself being ushered out and again into one of Signor Liskau's elegant touring-cars.

The seat was comfy, and I had nothing against this guy. He didn't resemble an ex-SAS gelignite expert and was hardly the source of my troubles, so far as I knew. Did I even have troubles? A half-fried face is far from a whole destiny. Why struggle, I thought as the Grand Corniche passed, like a shadow of glorious days. All would be explained in the long run, or at least something.

This was the line of the factotum, the Lancia whisking me back to pre-history – i.e., Liskau's place above Fontvieille. Was it possible that everything since my last visit had been but a dream?

'You're lucky you weren't burnt to a crisp in a Citroën,' was her riff, delivered in that grating chirp that made you wonder if she might have preferred otherwise. 'You're not six feet under, thanks to somebody. But you may be skating on thin ice.'

'Nice. I like mixed clichés. So this century.'

We were alone again, on that lovely terrace where poplar and umbrella pine framed and shaded afternoon above vast, cloudless striations of blue over blue. A servant loomed up, similar to or maybe the same as who had served me on the prior occasion.

'Tea, coffee, drink?' asked my hostess.

'You chose. Strychnine and soda's my favourite.'

She gave me a north of Boston glare. 'You're right – I don't like you. You're a fuck-up. Drink or no? Say. We don't have much time.'

'We never do.'

'Thé pour deux s'il vous plait,' she said to the man, who, shrivelling, dematerialized.

'Wellesley French?' I wondered.

'I went to Radcliffe, if you need to know.'

I knew from a year of frosh antics at Harvard that Radcliffe as such hadn't existed since days when her mother had been sewing mittens in upstate Vermont. But why quibble.

'One question further?' I asked.

She was about to sock me with the I-ask-the-questions-here routine but held back. 'OK. One.'

I gazed at the horizon, where turquoise kissed azure. The west would be one long *son et lumière* of freshening breeze and deep glows in a hour. It would have been heaven just to relax into it, but...

'Well?' she demanded.

'Can't you just pause for five minutes and live?'

Flipping her mane, she let out a nicker. 'Is that your question?'

'It is a question – existential question, if you had time for anything so beneath the Langley VA salt. But for these purposes we can call it rhetorical. No, my question is this: why all the B-movie tripe, explosions and so on?'

It was no good pushing rhetoric. 'What's the CIA got to do with the price of eggs?' – She was furious as a bourgeoise who's been overcharged for a sprout. 'I'm trying to help you, or somebody is; but frankly my patience is wearing thin.'

'You mean it was once plump and frisky?'

'Just like your father,' she hissed, spilling a bean. 'Sexist and crude to the core.'

'My core's like blancmange; gets more so every year. And why bring Dad into it? Did you know him?'

'Oh brother!' She coloured. – Blame it on tea, which arrived.

'I'm not your brother,' I returned, helping myself to a cup as weightless as silk. 'As to my father: the one I knew for more than for an hour was step, so we'd have to go into the Environment vs Genes trip to decide who's "just like" what; and I doubt your stuffed agenda would accommodate that... Biscuit?'

'Never.'

'Slimming?' – She was borderline anorexic.

'Cut the personal stuff, guy.'

'Cucumber sannie?'

'From *Playback* to *The Importance of Being Earnest* in a bound?'

'So you *did* go to college. And yes, earnestness might work. But you haven't shown any.'

She set her cup down and poured another. 'You have?'

'What about the big bangs?'

She seemed to go serious for half a second. 'Maybe someone's trying to send a message.'

'To who?'

'You mean "to whom".'

Our eyes locked. You might think each was thinking that he/she knew what the other was up to, but my guess is that you'd be wrong. If she were trying to send *me* a message, she'd have to be more explicit.

'Get it?' she punctuated.

'No.'

'O brother!' – not *O for fuck's sake*, though it's what I almost heard. 'Well, get this: someone may be thinking you know too much, or will. Someone may be saying in the kindest way to back off.'

'Treading on toes, am I?'

'You're getting warm.'

'Somebody's dreams?'

'Warmer still.'

'Yeah? You mean you know what's what?'

'I'm sitting here, aren't I?'

She pinged her cup on its saucer and for the first time looked as if a green demon weren't pinching her gizzard. Uncrossing her legs, which had braided in that twist only the brittle can do, she made you wonder if she were going to *smile*. There seemed danger of it, though, as I stared, something else seemed to swim into view: Sappho's island way out upon those storied seas. I detected a chance, just a hint, that she was going to frisk me for what I knew, or she sensed I did, about a more famous body. It was pleasant, if creepy, this competitive, faintly homoerotic tic you sometimes picked up off the type. I'd come across it before, recently at Alexandra's, night of the fire. It had hung in the air there, around the unattached dames. It had hung in the air in general, I realized, over Alexandra's scene in the years I had known it. 'Too much sex here,' one of Dad's pals used to say of Hollywood of his day; 'gets to be like flypaper, everything sticks, more and more stuck all the time, too messy...' A few decades on and Hollywood was the world, or at least London in my ken. But to be getting this vibe off an heiress to the puritan ages seemed like a downfall.

'So you are,' I replied, evading a glimpse up a culotte.

The calf failed to braid itself around its partner as its twin had. Sighing, she adopted a faraway look, as if she *were* about to take my advice and 'live for five minutes'. – Quelle prospect! But for me, it was nix. The actress at least had some idea of what a soul was.

I stood. She looked non-plussed.

'Gotta run,' I quipped. – Her face broke into a mid-period Picasso. 'Late for a date, just like Brer Rabbit. Or was it the Mad Hatter?'

She recovered and, back on familiar turf, snapped, '*Alice in Wonderland* now, is it?'

'Apparently, it always was.'

Not to miss a last word, she threw at my departing backside, 'Just remember this, pal – '

'"You can run but you can't hide"?'

That morphed her into one of the Eumenides. 'Something like that,' a voice spattered.

8.

I'd taken little or nothing from this strange interlude. Or had I? What had she told me? like Mazandaran, to back off? But had she? Had Alexandra? Had anyone? – I strolled over the Place in front of the Prince's toy palace, hearing again 'You know too much.' What, for example? That an actress was promiscuous? who would've guessed. That an L.A. wide-boy wanted a club in St Trop? quelle scandale. You have to do better than that, Dad on my shoulder was saying; have to get back to first base before you try to steal second. My problem? I could hardly see what or where first base was.

Past welded cannonballs and the Grimaldi archway, I hung like a tourist from Warsaw to gaze down over what Ranier and Grace had built. Purists say it is tacky – Miami on the Med and so on – but I liked it, this wedding of Modernism with *fin-de-siècle*; and the corniche behind all seemed to make man's disfigurings somehow less impious. Ranier and Grace: the Irish-American hod-carrier's daughter and Italo-Semitic scion of demi-usurpers... What came together to make this region tick? I was almost getting wise as I dropped down into La Condamine and sauntered across its market square.

Here you could rest unaware of the Anglos and Arabs, Russians and whomever who made port and high-rises thrive. Here something reliable and permanent lurked in an un-trafficked back street, little restaurant, bon marché hotel. Should I clear out of Cannes and come here? The thought brought me on to a difficulty: how do you check into such a security-conscious place without passport?

The factotum's tea having passed through, I experienced a fall. The shadow of the Rock blocking sun by the port may have been part of it, despite gold lighting the hill of Monte Carlo beyond. No passport? That could be taken care of with a phonecall. But a car blown? two cars? When would the flics be onto me? Sooner or later I'd pop up on an official screen, and there would be no actress to whisk down in a Liskau Lancia to spirit me off.

Spirit me... There had been the Alfa guy hours before, then the Lancia, one handing me over to the other. Why? What connection? How to connect? Actress, Mazandaran, Liskau, Alexandra's boys...

I was shuffling pieces as sun re-emerged east of port. Gazing onto the hulls and the masts, I thought: too bad Loretta wasn't there. The face of Jimmy came back, mild as evening breeze, distant as light. It made me re-ponder: was this boy at the heart of it somehow? this sprite whom a Shakespeare might have called a changeling? this weird, earthly embodiment of Ariel?

The idea, eccentric, vanished as soon as it rose, on the breath of the regret that she wasn't there. I turned back to the Rock and, crossing the traffic, went up to a chapel beyond which glass doors opened onto a lift that whooshed you up to a platform and, in my case, the next the train back to Cannes...

My room had been ransacked – that figured, huh? Downstairs a dusky face hardly left TV to track me – figured too. What was I to deduce from it? that he was in cahoots? it was Ayrabs what done it, masterminded by Zabiha from Beirut? Whatever, it seemed time to get out of there. So clad in my worst, backpacked like a deadbeat train-bomber, I checked out and traced steps down to the Croisette.

It was evening now, lights starting to flick on, casting their Hopper-esque shadows. I felt a twinge of something – *amour de l'impossible,* though for what I wasn't sure. I'd been alive half a century nearly. It's easy to know what you want when you're young: if in a week or a year it should change, that hardly matters. But by the time you got to my age, too many false grails had been found for you to be quite sure you still knew what was meant by the quest. Even so, you kept searching, kept yearning – and that was the secret, wasn't it? the one Dad never let on about. That's what kept it all going, until it didn't, even for a half beaten-up old timer like him, or now me.

Steps leading down to the east side of port... Liskau's yacht – it was *there*! I stared, stupefied. Logic would put it off, say, Costa Smeralda by now. So: was anyone on it? Not a light. Not a sound.

Circumnavigating, I went to the place where I might get explanation. But the Timer's slip was as empty as a child-snatchee's crib. Again, why? *That* vessel hadn't budged for years by his word.

No one was in either craft alongside to shed light. I went to the capitanerie but, it being past sunset, got only a tip to come back in the a.m., ask the *chef*. A thought came that the old guy couldn't have gone far in a tub in the shape of his, so I put to the Gitane-puffer on duty,

'Ou est l'endroit plus près pour reparations?'

'Mandelieu,' this one grumped. 'Oui, c'est possible. Logique ça.'

These petits fonctionnaires in their *sangfroid*... Recalling the old guy's regard for French authorities, I hailed a cab.

Mandelieu being not far, I discovered shortly that he wasn't there either, nor had been, nor was expected. So was it possible he'd cast off for the Blessed Isles? 'Too much for me now...' Had he cleared out of Cannes in some kind of panic? If so, over what?

Loretta – 'like a daughter to me'... Why had Liskau's boat been in the harbour and she not on it? Yes, Loretta... 'C'est un autre endroit pour reparations près d'ici? Pas plus loin de Cannes?'

Villefranche, I was told – and jumped for it. *She* wasn't one to go to sea in a tub in the shape of the Timer's. Besides, wasn't Villefranche in her word 'one of the prettiest' spots on the coast?

It wasn't late – a train or two more till the last, Marseilles to Ventimille… From the station, I went down a flight of stone stairs, saw the lights over the Welcome, thought of Cocteau and Maugham on the Cap. Did some sweet scent pervade the place because of her liking for it, or was I just picking up on a sense that – hugged by the corniche and arms of the port – Villefranche held a quiet that made it seem unlikely to be prey to the fate of Nice and the rest?

Deep in well of the harbour where repair yards sat, a Renault rental van was pulled up. 'That you, Pop?' I chirped, locating my quarry.

His tub was moored to the quay, he lugging items from it. 'Who's that?' he gruffed, joy unreciprocated.

'Just one of the youngsters, hoping for a cuppa.'

He squinted, then popped eyes. 'Get out of here.'

Mistaking this for some cantankerous endearment, I said, 'Looked for you in Cannes harbour. I was half-worried you'd set sail for the Land beyond the Western Wave.'

'Git!' he repeated – no endearment, after all – 'or you may never have the chance.' With that he reached into the cab of his van and pulled out what Dad might have identified as a Battle of the Bulge vintage Luger. 'I'll give you the count of three.'

'Come on, man. I'll give you the count of Monte Cristo. You're not going to fire that.' – But he did.

It had a silencer on it and was not aimed exactly. The thud of its bullet produced no heads-up from anywhere in that mild paradise. Back on the esplanade a clatter of dishes and mo-peds could kill any sound at such distance. Off in deep waters a naval frigate or two would absorb whatever carried as no more than the backfiring of a constipated Peugeot up on the corniche. I was cornered, and this old man's benignity had turned malicious.

'Now git, little double-man, whoever you work for.'

Fool me! If Emily Dickinson could become a thug, why should Pa Joad remain the salt o' the earth? *That* was the message. I was getting it now loud and clear. Fuck my father, it almost made me think truly for the first time: the hell with his era's sentimental affection for Red Noorgaard and kind! But then... the sound of a voice like a castrato's rose, as if out of an air out of Händel. Towards the boat's cabin the Timer's eye flicked, and as the sound died into sing-song – contented, indecipherable – I grabbed for the gun.

He couldn't pull back quick enough to keep my hand from twisting. His grip was the stronger, old knot-raveller that he was; but I had thirty years on him. An uneven contest was just turning my way when, words preceding body, Loretta emerged onto deck:

'I thought I heard voices. Is something wrong?'

Wrenching the gun loose, I let his wrist drop. She stared at me, at him, at me; almost smiled, frowned.

'Why are you here?' she wondered.

'Why are you?'

The old guy grunted, grumbled, threatened things rash. She looked, listened a beat more, then said:

'You take care of Jimmy, Dad. I'll handle this.' – Without further ado, she put a hand out for the gun.

How could she know that I'd turn it over? How could I know that it didn't matter if I did? Well, you have to trust someone. And since she evidently trusted this old cuss with the most precious thing on earth to her, that boy, why shouldn't I put faith in her?

I gave up the gun, its owner still all grumbles and mutters, cross as hell. 'Back in twenty,' she concluded and, beckoning me with a look, headed off into the lights.

At the edge of the square before you dropped down to the Welcome, she indicated a turn. In we went to a bar, hardly inhabited, nondescript. 'Deux pressions,' she called to the moustachioed tender and seated herself in a booth. I did likewise. He came, served.

She said: 'I don't know you. I met you on Giovanni's boat. Are you working for him?'

'Do I look like it?'

'You said Alexandra sent you that time. I believed you then. Has she sent you now?'

'No.'

'So why *are* you here?'

I felt heat rise, but it was too dim for her to see.

'I wanted to talk to you myself,' I answered.

I couldn't tell if she coloured. After a beat, she repeated, 'Why?'

'I'm not sure,' I said, though I was quite. 'Let's say I was worried.'

She absorbed that. 'How did you know?'

This threw me, but I ventured, 'Felt it.'

She nodded. We sipped.

'OK,' she went on. 'How much do you know?'

'Not a lot.'

'Did she say how we got here?'

'Does she know you're in Villefranche?'

'No one does, except you. And I've got to trust that you're not going to spill. Can I?'

'Have you got a choice?'

'We could blow you away.'

Our eyes locked. Hers were ringed, but not watering.

'I'd rather you didn't,' I gave back, trying to lighten it up. 'I'd rather you'd tell me what she never did when she roped me into this round of unclean situations in the first place. I guess you mean it in a larger sense: "How we got here"?'

She took a sip and half grinned. I recalled the look, and liked it. She shook her tight locks as if I, or she or both of us were damn fools:

'Gianni knew her before those boys were born; before she was married even. He'd known her husband; maybe introduced them – there was always something between them: the sort of confidence that goes way back with folks who've known each other since before they've become what they have. They kept in contact. She always wore his clothes, introduced him to bigwigs in London when she started getting a name. That's what it was like. Jimmy – James – when he came along with his brother was the love of her life. They were triplets to begin with; third one died. Age two or three, they diagnosed him with autism. Out of guilt maybe, it made her love him the more; but everyone else gave him a wide berth. You know how it is at that level in places like London: even his dad – a poet! – couldn't relate to a kid who was never going to go to the best schools or get on in ways "one is supposed to". Rafe was no problem: he had the right stuff; only his brother was James. But that's another story. Giovanni was one of the few who took to the kid. He loves beautiful things: that's his genius, a religion to him; and Jimmy… well, anyone with an ounce of imagination can see.'

'That he's Beauty incarnate?'

She drank. I did too.

'I don't have time to go into detail,' she went on after a beat. 'We're going to ground now. You were never here.'

'I'm your paladin, full-stop. But give me a bit more. Tell me while I walk you back to the boat.'

'You're not walking me back to the boat.'

'You think I'm scared of the Timer?'

She said emphatically, 'Don't!'

So I was stuck. 'OK. Your rules. But before you go… you don't need to say where you're going, but I'm a friend. Put me in the frame.'

She considered, then said, 'Time came, after their Dad died, useless though he was, and Raphael went to school, that Alexandra didn't know what to do. That's when I came in. Giovanni knew. He could see what was needed – light, air, wind, stars, illusion of freedom, whatever all this is you can get here and nowhere else. He had the boat already; I'd been looking after it for a year. So one day he gives me one of those long stares he does when he's sizing up a woman and says, "How would you like a cabin-boy, bella?" And once he'd explained and I'd said OK, it was up to Alexandra – and eventually Jimmy.'

'I see,' I said as she stood.

'But what went wrong?'

'I hadn't got there yet.'

'But you will. Something did. And you may be part of it. But I can't afford time to speculate. Sorry: I'd like to. We have to go.'

I went to the door with her. She whirled around.

'Don't follow. I mean it! And be careful. I like you.'

9.

The gaze held me. Like a deer in the glare of a headlamp, I watched her svelte form shrink into the cluster I knew to be that of the Timer, the Renault and Jimmy. She went down in the boat and came up more quickly than it takes a tear to dry. Before thirty seconds had passed, she was with them in the van, up the corniche and out of sight, though hardly of mind.

I strolled past the Welcome. 'Hey sailor,' someone called – the night was progressing. I strolled further on, past a last restaurant, along the side of the water, down to where stones rattled and shifted restlessly. It smelt fishy, damp, non-judgemental, familiar, like a place you could shiver the night away in and no one would tell you to get up, get going, get out or whatever the world said – our world, 'civilization'. But not this one. Not this older, duller, more endless, accepting, light-dappled darkness and brine… I wanted to plunge into it. But guess what, Dad? I was like you, and most of the others. I was not Jimmy; and maybe Jimmy wasn't Jimmy, as I imagined him. We all belonged to the big mess, human cluster, for better or worse. So, turning back from that ineffable sublime, I climbed the stone steps above town and re-entered the station.

No more trains east, just one more slow one west… I could've gone back and tried my licence at the Welcome, or 'Hello sailor' might have impelled me as far as Marseilles. But considering my present situation, not to mention how I was feeling, I stepped on board and, when St Raphaël came, stepped off again.

It was past midnight. Where go? A café off the main square was lit, side street, direction of beach. I sat in it an hour, atmosphere French, ordinary. A barmaid nice-looking in a sharp, unpretentious way – peroxide hair, OK curves, faint reminiscence of some small town on the Southern Cal coast of the '60s… Time wound down gently. I was teenaged again, half-hopeful, despondent. It was easy to want her to gaze back as she went round closing the place. If I smiled, said the right word, might she have offered a couch for the night?

It was like that – freedom – a certain kind of France. So why spoil it? Ambling down to port, I found a crook in a seawall and lolled against my backpack to wait for dawn and a first boat over the Golfe. Breeze through the cables crooned lullabies; water swished soft against a landing-bay. Light came up slowly, blue turning orange, silhouetting church towers. A café opened and disgorged its first espresso et croissant to Dad's unknown aficionado of Jack Kerouac.

Boats waking, a ferry showed. So, in due course, wind scatting my hair, I watched new day glittering over our wake and a St Raphaël more picturesque than the real one receding before and behind me.

At St Trop I wound up to an alley behind Place des Lices and rented a scooter. Maybe the night rough had made me fearless. Whatever, I took off without second thought about where I was headed and, after a number of roundabouts, was again facing PROIE.

No life. Too early. The Maso had been removed, its carcass anyhow; where it had been was a divot as if dug by the Jolly Green Giant. Was that why they'd closed him down before he'd begun? Above the doors was a St Andrew's cross of yellow tape. Below it hung a scrap of yesterday's *Var Matin*: 'Presqu'Île,' read the runner: 'Blitz de vigilance: manque de licence.' A headline: 'Nouveau Club non in régle. Fermeture jusqu'à compliance pour equipe californienne.'

Well, well. A smiling mug – our Sammy's – was set like a dark diamond in the midst of two columns explaining how, despite unexpected delay, the most hip of new venues for the Juicy Groove set was to be up and running by summer season.

'Good reading, pal?' a voice at my back sarked.

I turned to peer into the browned chicklets of Dewey.

'Hey, ho-dad. What's the haps?'

The grin went shit-eating. 'Cowabunga. It's you!'

'You thought I was stardust with a Maso? Well, don't be sad. There's my new motor; why not try again? Or for the third time – cute little Citroën. Was it you?'

He gave me the scowl these medium toughs favour, the ones with small minds and big pecs. Meanwhile round a corner sauntered my friend of the day before, the one in shades who liked Occitan tunes.

'Problème?' he inquired.

'Problem? Problem, all right,' Dewey went. – I use Valley syntax.

'Et vous?' asked the other.

'Je cherche Monsieur Mazandaran. Est-il disponible?'

'"Ay teel disponeeble",' mimicked Tarzana's best. 'Who're you kidding, pal?'

My Occitan guy gave me as close to a smile as he had in the rep. Motioning me to follow, he made for his Alfa, parked a storefront away. Climbing in, he flicked t-spark. I swung a leg over my scooter.

'Think you're a smart-ass, don't you?' Dewey snarled. 'You're the worst kind, fag boy. Remember what they used to say?'

'No, but you're going to remind me.'

'America, love it or leave it,' he grunted, confirming a mindset bred in the era of Spiro T. Agnew.

Fortunately, I didn't have to consider those options now. The Alfa smoothed off; I fired up, puttered into its wake and was soon in the company of Mazandaran and his retinue of the hour:

They were sprawled on long, low, white sofas at the Cinquante Cinq. Pamplonne beach lay pristine in the background. Weeks prior to crowds, the chic bar of the past decade looked as if it had opened solely out of courtesy to this wounded New Kid in Town.

'Gonna buy the place, Sammy?' one of the t-shirts drawled.

''s where the action is,' teased another. 'No shtick over licences.'

A couple of chuckles, ignored by the boss.

'We could make it better,' he mused, scanning the horizon as if an authentic heir to transcendentalist visionaries. 'There's a nude beach down there – place is Topanga before L.A. got wise. We could clean it up, create a luxury brand, new formula, tech savvy.'

'Right on, man!'

His court settled into chastened reverence as he swivelled shades, cool as Bonaparte assessing maréchals of the Grand Armée.

'Hey man, where's Philippe?'

'In town with San, trying to talk to somebody.'

'Yeah? Well, I hope he gets it across to these dudes – I'm a businessman, not a hippy. That old thing is like over! Left Bank, Bardot... We're talking well-designed spaces, humongous sound; a place on the map, centre of art, man, real culture; place people can get out, act like real city-dwellers, not stay-at-home creeps in the two-mill gated bunker kicking back to stare at a fuckin' oversized screen.'

'Right on!' – More tough-love affirmation.

'So, when'd they say they'd be back?'

''bout now.'

A head or two revolved towards deep rattan, a dark corner which served as exclusive entry to this venue otherwise accessible by naturists *en masse* off the sand. Out of its shadows I stepped, my Alfa guy now faded into a periphery of bamboo and pampas grass.

Mazandaran stared. One of his heavies raised an arm. The Cinquante Cinq tender moved as if to block me.

'Hey bro', 's OK.' boss man intervened. 'He's my cunt-cousin.'

To this prelude, how to react? The retinue with more swivels and flexes; Mazandaran with geniality and a frown – the sultan before he slices your head off.

'Hey guys, what about that place up the beach, far end, Tahiti? I want it checked too – better location, closer to town, nestled up in the rocks there… Go for it. Have a drink if it's open. Can't do squat here till San and Philippe show.'

They pulled their Gold's Gym bodies off cushions and in less time than it takes to pass wind were out of there.

'Nice way to ask 'em to scram,' I opened.

'Told you I was a sweetheart. Sit.'

'Don't mind if I do.'

So here we were again, Dad's two tough boys, ready to snot at one another across a table – in this case very low, the latest in beach chic.

He said nada. I offered no more. We stared at each other. Finally he gave a throat-clearing hack.

'Now you're going to ask me why I blew a Maso?'

'And C2.'

'I heard about that. A little, or not so little, black bird told me.'

'You like midnight-blue black birds.'

'I like birdies, true. Beautiful ones. Hawks, eagles, birds-of-prey… They come in many colours.'

'But dark, mostly.'

'Shows the dirt less.'

'Convenient.'

Shrugging, he gazed at the shore. This was the moment when one of Dad's heavies would light a fag and blow smoke in your face. But we were too green for that nowadays.

'What gives?' he asked after the scripted pause.

'OK, let's be direct. Did you do it to get me, out of jealousy – another message to "back off" – or is this to do with some larger scheme I don't know about?'

'How do I know what you know about, man? I know who you are but not who you *are*. You belong to that category Rumsfeld used to talk about during the Iraq gig: "the known unknown".'

'Or "unknown known"?'

'Clever. Point taken.'

'And leading nowhere. So let's get back to first... If it was you trying to blow me, here I am. My scooter's out there – like I told your surf friend, why not try again? See if this cat has nine lives.'

'The cat who walked backwards?'

I turned it over. 'It was *her* you were trying to send a message?'

'Maybe. And maybe she passed the poisoned fruit-tart to you.'

'And when I failed to gobble it down, someone served another?'

He shrugged. 'Looks that way, don't it?'

'It does. So?'

'Who dun it? I hate to disappoint you, pal, but that may just lead to another of Mr Rumsfeld's categories – the biggie.'

'Let me guess. You mean "the unknown unknown".'

'Now I can see why San's mama sent you.'

'And why your girlfriend went for me?'

The *faux*, if it had been, geniality faded. 'Careful. It still hurts.'

'But not enough for you to do her, or me.'

He evaded a direct answer. 'I loved that Maso... Baby Citroën?' He swatted an obliging mosquito, and we were left with him trying to stare me down. There was something childish in it, but I guess even Saddam Hussein must have been a kid once. 'Drink?' he inquired.

'What, dashed with ether?'

'Back to that, huh?'

'We started out on the wrong foot as I recall. Or was the

72

Billionaires' for my entertainment?'

'OK. Maybe we should try to get on the right one. Trouble is, like Rumsfeld with you old lefties and Euro-creeps, I don't know whose side you're on. You lived in my town once: you oughtta know better. Just because a guy talks like he's grown up with a Corleone spoon up his butt doesn't mean he can't be a straight businessman.'

He had a point there. And it *was* half a pleasure to engage in chat resembling one of Dad's old-time snarl-ins. So I accepted his offer. We ordered – orange pressé and lattè for him, espresso for me. Waiter dispatched, he turned shades to the sky, as if aesthetics were his sole occupation. Soft cello lead-in, and he was into the baritone aria:

'You came looking for San, right? Someone broke you into my apartment; I'd like to know who. Maybe you should too – maybe that's who's been sticking Roman candles up yours… San's facing this guy, weirdo, half-burned; says he comes from his mother, who he don't wanna see. Why? We'll get to that… It's my apartment, not his; he works for me and may be smart, but he's only a kid. There's someone else there too, always is. They hear voices, come, see what's up, act – not rough: we're not the Bugsy beat-the-shit-out-of-everyone-in-sight crew, but we gotta defend ourselves, right? You go crash – out like this place when winter comes. Who are you? You got some ID, but no local address. Where're we s'posed to send the package back to? London? Hey, I got enough troubles without trying to kidnap some gremlin onto a flight – not even Easyair, or whatever.'

I nodded. After a moment of weighing it up, I said:

'If you wanted to find out who got me in there, why not just tie me up to a chair and slap it out of me?'

'Like Clooney in *Syriana*, eh? But like I told you, pal: just because I come from L.A. and my father grew up in Tehran or wherever doesn't mean I do torture.'

'Maybe not. What about Dewey and José?'

'Those guys…' He waved it off. 'High-school parking-lot stuff. No finesse for nail-pulling.'

'Yeah, unskilled labour… OK, taking it your route, if I believe it, what happened? I passed out?'

'You were gone, man – that's what San says. I wasn't around –

bankers' shit; meetings. They didn't know what to do, so they helped you to sleep till I showed. That's all. Ain't no biggie.'

'Not to you. And the Billionaires'?'

'Drunks stagger in with their friends, pass out in a booth, get dished to the bulls smelling drunker.'

'Or with a bouncer, bribed?'

'Never.'

'No, you're a girl scout. So's the actress. By the way, was she part of your performance, or was that her own improvisation?'

'She was there to meet me, last minute deal. I had another meeting; 'sides, it wouldn't've looked good for me to show while my guys were taking care of you. They're nobody. People recognize me.'

'I saw yesterday's paper.'

He spanked another obliging mosquito. 'Don't believe everything you read. Do I look like some small-timer worried about passing another five grand to some crap *fonctionnaire* for a liquor licence?'

'I wouldn't know. I don't know many guys like you.'

He half-grinned. 'The're not many.'

'Appears to be some competition here.'

'Not in my league, babe. I'm an *artiste*.'

'And about to remake the little corporal's empire – I heard. Was it why Josephine was in such a rush to see you? "last minute deal"?'

A frown crumpled what had almost been a smile. 'It still hurts.'

'Sometimes pulling on it gives a nice ache.'

Drinks came. He took a sip of his pressé, winced, grabbed for sugar. 'We got more to talk about? If not…'

'What's the rush?' – I quaffed mine straight. 'Philippe's still not here, nor the one you call San. I'd still like to see him.'

He sweetened his; it seemed to help. 'Why?'

'Why not? Can't he speak for himself?'

'I already told you what happened.'

'O I don't care about that. I don't even care about your actress, though there're still questions – such as, if you or Dewey didn't blow her Maso, who did?'

He shrugged. 'Maybe her. Maybe she wanted to get rid of the taste of a big error of judgment she made late one night after a hard day at – '

'Gianni Liskau's yacht? Joe, as she calls him?'

He went *stumm*. Sipped his latté – milk after citrus, bad combo. His cheeks frogged out/in, suppressing a burp. Mouth pursed, the look recalled George W. Bush. So was this the story? Was he just one more would-be hard rich kid? a Dodi Fayed who'd backed a few indie films and fancied himself in the big game as a result? Clearly someone thought so: the liquor licence fracas proved it. Did others take him for a touch: one or two Parisian designers maybe? What was this guy at core? Jay Gatsby trying to impress Daisy Buchanan-as-actress?

'Let's forget her for now,' is how I resumed when he failed to react to the name of Liskau. 'What I'm really concerned with is Rafe, "San". How is it he comes to be working for someone like you?'

'Ask him. But like I said: he don't want to chit-chat.'

'I'm not doing this for his Mom anymore.' I pointed out. 'I'm in it for myself now.'

'Yeah? Well, what does that make you? some kind of daddy-pederast creep? I think I've had enough of your kind for one a.m., pal.' – Placing his cup on it saucer, he let off another volley of burps. 'Why not take a hike down the beach, thataway. You might find some queer bait there to suit you.'

I'd had enough of myself in this pose too. 'Don't be a hog, Sam. I can't be boffing your gal *and* looking to pack toffee.'

'No? I thought you were one of those dudes could walk and chew spearmint at the same time.'

'Tough. But a man can only try.'

'Good. Walking's the first part. So blow.'

10.

It was kind of fun, Dad, till I got to the car park. There sat little moped with both tires slashed. High-school pranksterism indeed.

'Hey gremmie,' called Dewey, slouched in Jackie Kool posture against the rump of an Alfa. 'How they hangin'?'

He chortled himself silly as I inhaled dust, making my way up towards the Route des Plages.

It wasn't hard to hitchhike into town. France was not yet a country where people that looked like I did were a cause for steep acceleration. I might have used the time better, but it was nice to discover one or two souls that were still sympathetic.

At the bike shop they gave me a new Vespa, apologized for the delinquency of locals and said they'd send someone collect flat-tired *motopied*. I didn't complicate matters by saying it wasn't a local who dun it: there's National Front in the Var, and conclusions might have been drawn before my schoolboy French could dispel them.

Like San Francisco or Venice, St Tropez has a finite charm. So despite its encrustation of tourists, inevitable steps led me down to the old town and port. Barely June still, it was quiet, clean and as native as could be given a lifeblood of richies off yachts, *rentiers,* day-trippers arriving to ogle. The morning was fresh, light gold on tile roofs, air not yet too stifling. I was happy, I realized in one of those accesses you have of being alive. So when I caught sight of Rafe in Le Gorille, my instinct was simply to loiter and look.

What I saw was a young man much like I'd been once, student-type bent over papers, plans – you couldn't read what lay on the table but could guess. There too, somewhat older, was the designer Philippe, if that's what he was called. He gestured, explained things while the boy listened, nodding, occasionally scribbling a note. Energy was in him, and the conversation. Inspiration seeped around them, like sun through the flap separating the café from a bar-tabac next door. The boy was doing something, creating something; and it told a tale. Sam Mazandaran, whatever else he was, had offered this post-teen a chance; and he was taking to it with zest.

Light dappled the space by the bollard where I lounged, dockside of the water. Should I disturb them? No reason. Here was a young man on his way: if he didn't want to be reminded of whatever drama he'd come from, that was his call. Why Alexandra should have asked me to find him returned, puzzling. The fact that she had no direct access to him seemed further reason to lay off. Be yourself, kid, I found myself saying inwardly and with a pang recalled something good in my past that, before it had quite formed up, dissolved, leaving only the rind of a vision of what might have been.

Alexandra should've told me more – really she should have. I passed an internet café and thought of emailing her before realizing that she was the kind who'd barely made it into the age of the fax. *Email* no doubt conjured some witty remark about splitting the distance between genders. The whole set was like that. Edward may have had a IT girl to do for him; Luther too, RIP. Zabiha, being foreign, peripatetic and hungry may have come up to date, also the unattached dames and young neo-con, though affectation would have made him appear to disdain it. In short, I had no one to text to shed light on this kid. Still, internet gets you Google. So I went in, paid my euro and sat down to try to pull up another scrap of the picture:

Giovanni Liskau – thousands of entries – too many. So were the fogies right? did this new tech get you nowhere? Website, grand openings, *couture* shows, special offers... somewhere I clicked on an article translated into a dozen languages. It must have been recent because it told of his yacht and palaces in Monaco, Rome, Santa Margherita, Paris, Holland Park. There was a photo – mug shot as if for passport or police. It made him look like he wore contacts, had had a nose job, a hair transplant, a tuck beneath one eye and botox or whatever that stuff is that pumps out the cheeks. He looked phoney, in a word. But GL was high glam. Sam Mazandaran seemed like the unwashed off the mean streets by contrast. Who knows? Maybe he was.

Research raising little, I took a spin on my Vespa. Doing the roundabouts, I veered through Plan de la Tour. It was a fine day, verdant, clean as a Bonnard varnished to be put up for sale at Christie's; which reminded me... Alexandra's may have been quicker on a Harley, but what was time to me now? What was it to anyone, I might have thought on arriving; because no one was there, nothing had been touched, not a wall demolished, let alone rebuilt. There was no sign that a crew had even set down a tool. The ruin remained ruin, looking for the life of it as if it had no future but abject neglect.

So what *of* that Bonnard I had seen in her hallway? What about other artworks, the many dotted around in that tipsy way the English affect, or used to, to assure the world that they have no taint of pretension? All gone now. Vanished. Had they been burnt? If so, how many? Were they insured? If so, for how much?

This wasn't my remit either. On the other hand, I remembered a squall late in the life of a previous Anglo here, re an auction whose proceeds were meant for a last catamite rather than un-doting daughter. Irrelevant, maybe – Somerset Maugham was hardly Alexandra, though her husband had known him and debunked him like the rest: a bestseller who'd had the temerity to acquire stockbroker millions. Not that her husband had been poverty-stricken – far from it. But *his* wealth, such as it was, had come from land, title and perks stretching so far back that no one could recall how it had been come by; and his writing occupied the slot such excrescences should in the eyes of that set – as *jeu d'esprit,* not commercial effort.

Sitting on her terrace, I pondered these sociological details. It was one of those moments when Maigret, alone at Quai des Orfèvres, might have lit up a pipe and considered joining Janvier or Lucas down at the zinc-top for a demi. But before I got far into that reverie, it was interrupted by a rattle of stones up the drive; and into my vista, abstract or real, purred one of those tasteful grey Lancias that could mean only Liskau and Co.

The sight of my scooter halted it. I was hardly trying to hide in an orchard, and whoever was in the car must have spotted me, because when a door opened it was only one and in back. Out stepped the factotum. A slight hesitation, and she made straight for me.

No gun was in her hand, but her eyes were sited like barrels: black, close together. 'What are you doing here?' they shot.

'Same question. I didn't know you knew where *here* was.'

'Of course I did. Do.'

'Right. You know everything. Or your sources.'

'My sources have nothing to do with you, guy.'

'What a relief for national security.'

She put a hand to each hip, if that's what you could call those escarpments. 'I thought I told you – '

'That someone was trying to send me a message?' – I ticked my pate towards the ruin. 'Were you trying to send Alexandra one too?'

She spun on her pins and gestured to the car. The driver's door opened, and out stepped a suit. If there was another one in back, it kept behind tinted glass.

'OK wiseacre,' she tossed at me, 'I'll level with you. Alexandra's boy has gone missing.'

The driver, reaching the edge of the terrace, halted for instruction. He was the same who had relayed me from Occitan man, but neither of us indicated acquaintance. 'Am I to take it that's why you're here?' I asked, rolling eyes back to Miss Tough Gal.

'What else would it be?'

'To check out real estate?'

Her barrels twitched like a gunsel's trigger finger. 'Bluff!' she spattered. 'Wisecracking, warmed-over misogynist insinuation! I've had enough of it, fella.'

'I like you too,' I cheesed. 'And Alexandra's not here, by the way, if that's who you were expecting.'

'Why?' she demanded.

'Why would you be expecting her? You didn't just come to tell *me* James had gone missing?'

The barrels grew gables. 'You already knew?'

'Knew what?'

'Too much. Like I told you the other day.'

'How time flies when you're having – '

'That actress? Hey, there'll always be chumps in the world. But Loretta? And why *you*?'

'Good question. Best in the book so far.'

The gables flattened. A new look to kill. Then she spun again to hurl at the driver: 'Take him. And don't let him see where.'

It wasn't one of those Klan hoods like they used in Abu Ghraib, only the sheerest of GL scarves; but it worked. I couldn't see who the mystery guy in back was, if there was one; and by the time we'd got somewhere, I'd been out to the count for – well, you tell me.

Ether again or just one more of those concussive lapses meant to have ripped an afternoon from my life days before? Whichever, I have to admit that it was preferable to being nabbed as a frat pledge, flown to the Yolo Bolly Mountains, dropped in my Fruit-of-the-Looms and told to find my way home. I wasn't left to my wits and the kindness of strangers but shown to a room where linen slacks in my size had been laid out, along with a cashmere pullover.

Lamplight was low and day out the window died like a *bel canto* heroine. Cream silk in the room and coral blue out there made you dream of rich heavens – an eternity sprinkled with points of light from pale stars; a paradise where effortless eroticism could whisper and flow beyond end into the still pools of Lethe.

I was consumed by nostalgia. For what? Was it some drug they'd transported me on, or a tendency in me already? Whichever, I peeled off my dead mufti, showered, shaved and, scenting myself, dressed in the sleek duds to slip out into vague sounds of trad jazz and soft rock that snaked up a corridor padded in melon and pearl.

A party was in train, neither dinner nor drinks, a genial *va-et-vient*, soft-lit, glamorous, un-chatty compared to Alexandra's. This was Gianni Liskau's scene – not cleverness, beauty; not machismo, male or female, but serenity. I was put in mind again of some piquant vermouth, and such a refreshment was placed in my hand. The factotum was nowhere: she would never have fit among women who loomed up like shadows of goddesses projected through gauze, or young men who seemed to descend from marbles by Praxiteles.

'I've lived for Beauty,' the designer breathed into my ear, surfacing. 'Is it wrong? An old English novelist I used to know spoke of the Platonic virtues. There were three, he would say, the other two being Goodness and Truth. Truth is relative – we cannot rely on it. Beauty, though we love it, is evanescent and dies; alas, we may depend on that neither. Goodness in the end is all we are left with. So we must learn to be good in old age – it is our destiny.'

He looked like Aschenbach on the Lido: white suit, shirt with blue stripe, pink-and-grey regimental tie. The pigtail had been combed down to a duck on his nape; the ferret narrowness of features – reaction to sea air? – had relaxed. This enabled you to see that once, long ago, someone had bashed in his nose.

'I should say thank you for inviting me,' I put.

'The invitation may have been sent to an incorrect address – forgive. At any rate, you are here…' Wrapping an arm round my hand, the one that hadn't been scorched, he added, 'Come. Let me introduce you to some nice people.'

'I'd rather talk.'

'We shall have time for that later.'

'I'd like to now.'

He gazed at the tableau in his sitting-room – elegance as if spread out for a De Chirico painting. Beyond the grand windows hung a panorama of what I guessed to be Rapallo, sparkling into night aspect. Lights ribboned the bay, catching a mast here and there. The three of his yacht were not among them.

'We shall have fireworks shortly. They prepare for festival next month; it would be a pity to miss it. But perhaps you are right: if we talk now, we may enjoy ourselves later.'

He led me on a few steps and, dropping my hand, gestured to a door, which he opened. This led into a chamber festooned with fabric sufficient to upholster all the ladies-in-waiting to the Queen.

'You must excuse me.' – He teared up. 'It was Maman's day room. She's been with the puttis a year now.'

Indicating a sofa, he threw back a dust-cover to reveal more cream-and-beige. 'You must feel wretched. Was she terribly old?'

His mouth tightened: a cat's bumhole, not pretty. But no one like Liskau wants to show offence for long. The feline mask was back in place by the time we'd both settled.

'Mothers are our burden, whatever their age. To try to assuage their irrefragable anguish is what, in the end, we are about. That is our Goodness. Our medicament is Beauty… This was her house.'

'Nice. You must have loved her a lot.'

'"A lot", sir? Ah. Yes, I see what you mean. It was my way of showing her, after all those years, respect.'

'"All those years"?'

'Of poverty, starvation. I was born during the fascist times, war. It was not like it is now.'

'There are wars now.'

'Too many to keep track of. Trifling by comparison. Turf-battles, you may call them.'

'Try telling that to the Lebanese.'

He shrugged. 'Beyrouth was lovely once. It shall be so again.'

'Little boys playing Lego? Knock it down to build it back up?'

'You are no fool, sir. It is how the world turns. We are old peoples, we Mediterraneans, very old; Levantines more than most. But I'm glad you mentioned boys. Just now it is what concerns us.'

'Precisely. Where is he?'

His pupils may have dilated: it was hard to say – skin under the brows drooped like a hip-hopper's drawers. So was he subtle enough to see through my feint?

'Are you suggesting that neither of us knows?' was his answer.

'I can only speak for myself. A person in your position might be better able to judge.'

'"A person in my position",' he nodded. 'And what might that be? Do you have any idea of what it takes to build up such an enterprise as I have? Does anyone?… One or two possibly. A half dozen.'

'Sam Mazandaran?' I ventured.

The eyes became holes. Deep within them flared gleams, like glints off of stones peering out of sockets on bronzes from Minoan Crete. 'What is *he* to you?' Liskau inquired.

'No one. And to you?'

'Less than that.'

'Is that true? Or is truth, as you've told me, in this case "relative"?'

'My dear man, if you don't mind me calling you that – and I'd like to – you are wearing my clothes and, if I may say so, looking the better for it. You are sitting in my house, or one of them – my houses – and will be offered every comfort here. I would rather not be unpleasant; I'm sure you can see the point. So let us end this *pas de deux* on an up-beat. Please inform me of anything you know about the whereabouts of Alexandra's lost boy.'

'Which one?'

'Which one what, sir?'

'There are two boys – at one time three.'

'Yes, he was "lost" too, in a sense – I see what you mean. No, I was speaking of – '

'Jimmy. Not the other.'

Cat's bumhole again. 'Of course not.'

A brief silence. 'I wonder why?'

More silence. 'I'm afraid I don't know what you're alluding to. What did the boy say?'

'Nothing. I haven't been able to talk with him.'

'Then what are you intimating? And be cautious, sir: stories are sometimes related, but a boy of barely twenty can be unreliable.'

'Boys of most ages can be.'

He decided to smile then, or fade into a reprise of some loftier impassivity. 'That is a truism.'

'I specialize in 'em.'

'A man of your wit? I would never have guessed. But you are American by origin? Ah, well. I lost my prejudices as a street boy in Naples. One does not forget such a life. Which returns us to the topic… Jimmy as we call him, has, I'm afraid, been kidnapped.'

'"Kidnapped"?'

'For a boy like him, one can use no other term.'

'And Loretta?'

'Gone too,' he mused, hardly raising a lash.

'Oh dear.'

'So one might say.'

'So I do. I liked her.'

'We could see that. It is why you are here.'

'Not just for my pretty face?'

'My dear man – and I'm determined to regard you as such – I would like you to come in with me, at least on this. Please: help me in locating them.'

Was that the reason he had had me abducted, or wanted me to believe? Well, after a time I acceded, or appeared to. It seemed like the right wheeze; besides, I liked it there. Who wouldn't have?

83

Fireworks had begun by the time we stepped out of Maman's salon and onto a lawn to gaze over the town and port. A warm breeze was passing, held high by a hill cresting behind us, before tumbling down to Portofino. Something mellifluous in the air – an element analogous, say, to the difference in sound between Italian and French – reminded you that you were elsewhere, subtly further east, moving into some realm beyond clear Western precision. For a moment I recalled Zabiha and a description of hers, of a valley in the Lebanon where every Spring a river ran red as if with the blood of Adonis, causing the god to be reborn in the minds of the folk. After hideous dismemberment, a fair world is remade…

Up went the rockets: blue, green, mauve, diamanté. Explosion after explosion festooned the skies with exotic palm fronds, headdresses of bead. Liskau's minions came out, murmuring wonder. They lingered awestruck, grew mesmerized, fell into slow couplings or triplings against the sea air, eventually wandered off; and what would transpire in many rooms would stay as veiled as what had gone on below deck that night on his yacht, or earlier still in a far wing of Alexandra's villa. Give this old type of European his due: discretion. Sam Mazandaran may have been able to create spaces in which all could be promised or, for all I knew, had. Gianni Liskau by contrast specialized in the erotic – that is, left to the imagination or soul the infinite pleasure of painting its own sacred or profane fantasies.

Nor was he naïve. He knew that before I left in the a.m. I'd need some further explanation, even hint of confession, to fix confidence in him. So after the fresh muffins and coffee had arrived, the berries and kiwis and exotic fruit, the journals and papers in four languages, a telephone rang and his voice, husky, asked if I'd be willing to come up for a chat before Victor or Louis ferried me back to my neglected Vespa.

'Ah St Tropez,' he sighed in the chamber at top where he held his levee in a bed that might have accommodated all the mistresses of Louis XV. 'I used to go there with friends when young. We would walk in the harbour and gaze at the yachts. I wanted one so, but now I tell you, if I had one, I'd be ashamed. They are so large, so shapeless, like so much of the new wealth in our world – simply vulgar.'

We could have traded generalizations like this until lunch; but he guessed that I was too Anglo-Saxon not to want to prick them and watch them go pop, and he was too much of a Platonist for that; so we got down to business. Maybe he had other things on his plate too then: I'd seen some types on my way up waiting with folders like Philippe's, plans to spread out on a coffee-table as they took the same macchiato and croissant I'd had. What were they? designs for GL's autumn collection? Should I have peered over a shoulder? – By the time the possibility recurred, I would be back at Alexandra's, spitting stones up her drive. Meanwhile, my attention here was absorbed by what my host was choosing to share with me: recollection of his early days when *her* husband, as he confided, had been his lover.

'It was an era – the '60s, Nureyev, Fonteyn... The Marquis du Rocher kept a house at Hyères where they came. He would come too, *il poeta*. Ah, exquisite! the art, the concerti. I was a no one – a rude boy from nowhere. But someone saw I had a flair for design...'

The scene had moved on: Paris, London, Manhattan... 'I knew Warhol, Mapplethorpe – you've seen their pictures along the staircase? To them I was a traditionalist always; my fauves, *mes impressionistes*, the marvellous Klimt...'

Whatever had passed between him and *il poeta* was in time subsumed in a marriage arranged between the man and his top model... 'People speak of sexuality as if it were all black-and-white, but palest grey is its colour – every artificer knows. Great Visconti and his *Morte in Venezia*; the pearl of the lagoon – *that* is the element we all escape out of, and disappear into.'

In time came the boys... 'How did it happen? I was not there. I went to christenings, birthdays – Holland Park affairs, rather dowdy. But we love the English – *need* them – don't we?'

At last, problems. 'You must know teenaged boys. My dear, she could not cope. So? She sent them to me.'

Here it got tricky: '"Them". You mean Raphael too?'

'She would never have allowed James on his own – nor could I have taken on such responsibility, not at first: not until he could come to feel comfortable among us, and there was Loretta.'

What had gone wrong then? Why did Rafe leave?

Liskau rose from his monogrammed sheets. A robe fell apart to reveal calves thin as curtain rails, brown as cork. 'My dear, you must ask him. But again I warn: the tale of a teenager is rarely reliable. The whole of my existence up to adulthood was simply lie after lie.'

'And since?'

'Ah, you must ask. But consider: how could one create a business worldwide unless he were able, when it matters, to treat fairly?'

It made sense. 'So this matters?'

'Raphael's departure was a blow. Jimmy by then had become like – a son to me.'

'I see.'

'Perhaps you do.' – He began to dress now, or to assess what he might take from his department-store of a wardrobe. 'Perhaps on the other hand you have, like so many, inexact fantasies.'

I let that pass. 'Their dad was your lover?'

He slipped a satin hanger off a padded rod. 'Their mother too, as it happens, though *brèvement*. Does it signify? The boy after all *is* autistic. And there are her wishes to be considered.'

'Alexandra's?'

'We were speaking of somebody else?'

If it occurred to me to ask about the actress then, the question disappeared under what seemed more pertinent. 'So Rafe left and you never understood why?'

'That is what I have indicated.'

'And now James is gone, with no explanation either?'

'That is the implication of my remarks.'

'And Loretta?'

He paused, balancing pink vs puce in the shirt stakes. 'The woman was a godsend. She knows the sea like Calypso and can hold on to a pretty boy like Aphrodite to Eros.'

I pondered what that might mean.

'My dear, what goes on in the heart is obscure – especially in women, even to a seasoned observer like me. Perhaps in her soul she too has become diseased by affection; surely she has come to love the boy much. Perhaps on the other hand, he…' The voice tapered off.

'Perhaps he what?'

'Perhaps – no, undoubtedly – he is a man in body, even if in mind he is permanently *distrait.*'

I turned it over. 'Are you suggesting – ?'

'I don't know. It is unknown. I find myself asking myself, and then looking to you.'

'Me?' I concluded.

'Whyever not? Like Alexandra, on instinct. But then she knew your father, or her husband did, *en passant*... I may have even met him myself on occasion, one time, or twice.'

11.

A launch at high speed ferried me back over the Ligurian Sea. That pale grey he had spoken of owned the sky, and plenty of thought was born out of it – too much to relate. Suffice it to say that I was set down at Golfe Juan like Bonaparte fleeing Elba, then sped by the now inevitable Lancia (new driver) up to Alexandra's.

Nothing had changed. A plastic recliner had missed me. I returned to it and repacked Maigret's theoretical pipe.

The crossing had taken hours; now it approached end of day. Silence, birds nesting, a moan of evening breeze... After the bump of the wavelets and growl of engine, I was struck by how peaceful it was. It came on you in a way that would never have been possible when Edward and Luther were chuntering on, as if naught but gossip or wit could matter. The land had reclaimed what was hers to begin with. I felt like her guest now truly, a thoroughly privileged one.

Was this ghoulish? Did I wish everyone gone so we could return to inhabiting nature like spirits, disembodied, apparent to not a soul but our own? Or would we have been? Couldn't you see in that gloaming a shape rise, like a face in a cloud? Wasn't that the lynx-woman slinking off towards a copse? Could it be the young neo-con, transformed into scampering Pan? Was this Luther as satyr? And what had become of the woman with salacious, simian lips? Where had they gone to? Were they here still? What *are* the dead in proximity to their passing? the vanished entirely? the disappeared wholly? If so, what came around me then was only in mind. But it came nonetheless.

The wind's moan seemed to say I owed something to someone.

Or was it intimating that I had choice? I could do something or not; appease troubled spirits or leave them to howl and dissipate into permanent non-remembrance – that true 'unknown unknown'. And what was the nature of *that*, I wondered: a place which would be mine too one day? In this weird transit of memory and self-knowledge, wasn't it all about Goodness and Truth in the end, as Liskau said?

The wind sighed, and I ambled. Here was a wide stretch of land, gentle, precious, divorced from all that gaudiness down on the coast, yet close enough to bear relation to it. What a prize, I reflected, thoughts veering back to this world: what an asset for Alexandra and her sons if they wanted to sell, what a refuge if not. Which thought brought me on to a wonder of what it must have been like for them when small boys. Wouldn't it have been a blessed place, especially for James, autism being what it is? the essential familiar? And for Rafe, if he had strong fraternal feeling: wouldn't it still seem a fail-safe? an assured space where, if all else collapsed, his incapable sibling might be able to live like a hillbilly in bliss? Here the world hardly mattered. What civilization demanded couldn't insist. So I saw in a new light why Alexandra had asked me to contact them, also what the fire may have signified – not for her or the dead so much as for them. The future here was their patrimony: to rebuild or to sell would touch only a decade or two in her life but would fix, or surely affect, an adulthood for them. So what would they be feeling about it?

That was one question. There were others, related and not: too many to catalogue and file in such sensual stillness; so many that I decided to find a bed to lie down on and let them sort themselves out in the warehouse of dreams. So, turning back, I groped on to the house, in and up into a room I had once slept in.

Not much seemed changed in that shadowy light. The bed I found almost by smell, as though my scent had never left it. Lying down, I recalled how I'd entered a fantasy-realm here, though not quite of what. Shapes emerged, ectoplasms of desire – my desires, whatever they'd been; those of others too, possibly. And wasn't that a route to knowledge? *their* desires, not mine? If I could catalogue *them*, wouldn't I be able to glean what had gone on that night?

Emanations arrived, extraneous or not so. I fell into a pool;

recalling Liskau's mention of 'Great Visconti', I entered a scene out of Mann's novel that had not made it into the film. It was a lurid *Walpurgisnacht* in Aschenbach's native mountains, near to his old summer home. A concatenation of horrors, sexy witches and devils showing their backsides, groaning and heaving and tearing flesh, Dionysian orgy ending in rape and blood-lust, all preceding and being preceded by the most idyllic of Venetian visions, at the Lido, beside that pale, implausibly calm sea… So why had the filmmaker suppressed this? It was extravagantly cinematic. Was there something in it linked to his own past that he felt compelled to hide away?

Dad wouldn't have gone in for such speculations, I knew. Meanwhile, as I drifted, the beasts began to walk backwards, phantom-like, out of mind. I must have been more tired from sea-air than I realized, because by the time I'd pulled myself out of that emptying pit, orange was starting to press purple up against black and velvet to take shape as emerald hills to the east.

Out a window I gazed, into slight mist, lying in what apparently had been half a boys' bunk. Shadows in the field in front of that copse recalled an illusion I'd had the morning of the fire: Zabiha coming in from dawn prayers. The glow intensifying burned at the crest; then sun was up golden, and out of bed I got, groggy, half-decided to stay put, like Balaam's ass, until God spoke. It was a hermit's paradise here, after all. Besides, if I were right and the place meant something to them, any of *them*, I was unlikely to be left for long on my own.

'Thought I'd find you here,' chirped my first visitor, trying her damnedest to be pleasant.

I was lolling on the recliner, breakfasting on a tin of Heinz beans and half-bottle of claret I'd found in the remains of a kitchen.

'You're working for GL too now, I hear.' – It was the factotum.

'From whom? Your "sources"?'

Her sockets tightened. It wasn't easy to hide a natural animus, but she tried. 'Look, we got off on a bad foot at first. Now – '

'Now you just want to roll up in my smelly sleeping-bag and whine like a cat in heat till next Thursday?'

That did it. 'Listen, you fake macho creep – '

'"Look"? "Listen"? Who's being macho, or anyhow as bossy as a dried-up brothel madam?'

OK, that went too far; and I won't try to justify it by noting how the type had always provoked me. As my old mama used to say when I was teenaged, it was up to me not to let 'em.

'Sorry,' I managed but, taking her advantage, she had already started to simper, 'What makes you hate me so much?'

'I don't hate you,' I came back with, maybe too quickly. 'I don't "hate" anybody.'

'Your dad did.'

'No he didn't. He despised. There's a difference.'

I let her chew on that. She asked for no gloss. And maybe she wasn't so bad after all, I found myself thinking again, or hoping, as, sniffing back suds, she helped herself to the other recliner: the one Alexandra had lain on days (or was it weeks?) before.

'No driver today?' – An upright Fiat Panda stood out in the poplars. 'Feeling brave, eh?'

Brittle features eked out a kind of grin. 'I trust you,' she said.

'Oh brother.'

Was she embarrassed? Unlikely. She looked away, contemplated some rubble, gave me pause to consider whether I should ask who the mystery guy in back had been, the one they had blindfolded me not to see. Or had no one been there? Wasn't I still off with the fairies? Would she have told me if there had been?

The day had turned heavier, as if Moroccan, mixed. 'So you're here again,' I said. 'Mind if I ask why?'

'To see you, obviously.'

'"Obviously"? But you can't have been sure I'd be here. I could've been in Marrakech, Essaouria…'

'Not you, fella. I took psychology at – '

'Radcliffe? Yeah. And wrote your thesis on what – Varieties of Theoretical Experience in William James?'

'What was yours? Varieties of Saying Nothing in *The Golden Bowl*?'

I clucked. She made that heroic effort to smile. 'Want a hit of claret?' I wondered, lifting the bottle, shoving my bean tin aside.

She took a swig. Quelle surprise! Had she once in some dim past attended a keg-party?

'So?' I repeated.

'So it's like this… Some of it you know, some you may've guessed. That actress? She was Mazandaran's girl, or he liked to think so, and she let him for the five minutes she's capable of. Then she up and split. Ran to GL – she's known him forever: he cultivates 'em like rare orchids; knows just what they want, what he wants, what everyone needs – that's his genius, or part of it. So he gave it to her, what she wanted. Then, being half a moron, she got scared. It got messy. She blew it big time – called Mazandaran back and jumped into that smelly sleeping-bag with you.'

'I've fumigated it since – hoping someone might care.'

'Maybe somebody would, but not her. The half of her that's not a moron's a maniac. Why else would she go with a jerk like him?'

'Or Yours Truly?'

She covered the apparent *faux-pas* by saying, 'We all have to have a holiday sometime. In your case it was to get the taste out of her mouth, or wherever. But then she panics over that too. She has to have freedom, *has* to be unattached – no man owning a piece of her, not even the most minor, "theoretical" one. So she did it.'

'Did which?'

'Fucked you. To get rid of the other.'

'And all the while I thought it was true love.'

'Don't kid me, guy.'

'Well, she *did* give me her Maso.'

'Right. Fixed to blow.'

'Meaning you think *she* fixed it?'

'Who else would've?'

'Mazandaran bought it for her.'

'Even better. She sends two messages in one: tells you both to go fuck yourselves.'

I took a sip. 'So if that were the case, O Delphic one, why did my little Citroën blow too? She wasn't out to snuff me, was she?'

'She was pissed: you played careless; she isn't used to that. But no, I'd say that that one was him.'

'Getting me back for peeping up her tutu?'

'Be serious, guy. He almost killed you.'

'Somebody may have. And it may have been him. And it may just have been someone wanting to scare shit out of me, which doesn't appear to have worked.'

'Maybe you're more of a hardass than we figured.'

'"We"?'

'It's a manner of speaking.'

'Yeah. I've heard it before. From Royals.'

I re-offered the bottle. She knew better by now.

'Where is she?' she demanded, downshifting tone.

'Where's who?'

'Loretta.'

'How would I know?'

'Aren't you looking for her?'

'Thinking about it. What's it to you?'

'Loretta means Jimmy.'

'And Jimmy?'

'What about him? He's missing too.'

'And what's that to you?'

'It's not to me, it's to GL; you know that. You're not tracking.'

'Possibly better than you think.'

'Oh brother!' she snorted; and our blessed moment had passed. Recognizing which, I concluded:

'Good luck to you. And thanks for looking me up.'

She hung there for a beat, then stood. Twisting her sharp shanks like a poem to petulance, she hurried off through the poplars to roar – such as it was possible – her little Panda away.

The next applicant at my office was big Sam Mazandaran himself. He came alone too, unusually, seeming almost shy. By now I had moved on to a glass of warm beer.

'Thought I'd find you here,' was his opener.

'Così fan tutti.'

He didn't like the sound of it. 'Wha'?'

'Italian. Mozart; Da Ponte. I thought a cultured dude like yourself might've gotten the ref.'

'Hey, man!' – He sat on the empty recliner, which collapsed, producing expletives.

'Be my guest. Make yourself comfortable.'

'*Your* guest?

'All right, Alexandra's. But she ain't around.'

'I know that,' he grumbled. 'You told me you weren't working for her anymore. So why're *you* here?'

'"Working for" her? I never said I'd begun. And you said "San" had no contact with her, so how is it you know where she is or not?'

'I guessed.'

'You just said you *knew*.'

'What's with you, pal? I'm trying my best to be friendly, but you… What is it? anti-Semit?'

'Gott in Himmel. Is that card going to be played?'

'Why not? I get it plenty. Anti-Iranian, anti-Middle East. Some folks even take me for an Arab.'

'But never Mexican?'

He whinnied bad-temperedly, wrestling the seat into place. 'You're kind of a creepo, aren't you?'

'Some seem to think. Sometimes I even think so myself, especially recently, when gazing into a mirror.'

He looked up and, as if for the first time noticing my face, said: 'Hey, man – sorry. Truce?'

'Forget it. More warm beer inside. Want some?'

'Shit, I almost forgot!' – He rose and, the recliner re-flattening, jogged down to *his* Alfa to come back with a thin box, which he opened to reveal half of an anchovy pizza. 'Thought you might be gettin' hungry,' he explained.

'But how could you know I was here? Or no: you "guessed".'

He dropped the box on a table from which my hostess had once picked up an *FT*. As he wrassled plastic again, I added:

'You didn't really come here to see me, did you?'

Pretending not to hear, he re-set himself. As if to catch his breath, he gazed at the landscape. 'Nice spot, man. You got taste.'

'She did. Or her husband.'

'Yeah?' – He helped himself to a cold, cheesy wedge.

'So what does San think?'

'About what?'

'This place, naturally.'

'Whacha think he thinks? Loves it. Who wouldn't?'

'Does he talk to you about it?'

'We don't go there. Family stuff. Deep emotions.'

'Yet you knew about something.'

He gave me the Robert De Niro scowl.

'"Daddy-figure pederasts" I think was the phrase.'

He dropped eyes to my trousers, an inadvertent male thing. 'Nice threads, for a hobo,' he covered.

'Aren't they? GL. Man himself gave 'em to me.'

'Yeah? And what else did he give you, or you him?'

'Aw, Sammy… And with you and I just about to embark on a beautiful friendship, cunt cozes as we are…'

That did it. You could see rage ripple his biceps, though a good ol' Hitlerian will held it down. 'Be careful, man,' came the warning.

'I know. "It still hurts".'

He glanced at me sidelong. 'You too?'

'Not like you, pal. I cry uncle. She's yours.'

'Yeah well… I wish it was that easy. Any rate I'm flying to L.A. tomorrow. We'll see.'

'Flying to L.A.?' – This was unexpected. 'Why?'

'To see her. What else were we talking about?'

'Oh, the cloud over that copse. The breeze back in those leaves. The way a eucalyptus swishes back and forth across itself… I mean, what about all those big plans you've got going here? Surely the crap *fonctionnaire* didn't refuse your backhander?'

He looked truly exasperated. 'Why be like this? We're on the same team, or oughtta be. You know the score: how they pretend to speak only French when the radio's blaring ZZ Top or the Stones. They play with me; play with my boys. I shoulda hired Moroccans.'

'It's not the era of Emperor Maxmilian,' I observed. 'The French have nothing against Mexicans that I know of.'

'Chicanos nowadays. You *have* been away.'

'I thought you said we were "on the same team".'

He stared at the vista, or maybe an inner one. 'You could help,' he muttered finally, low-voiced.

'Help? Hey, my command of the language is nowhere near as good as Rafe's – San's.'

'True. But he's young. Someone has to keep an eye on him.'

'The last time I tried that I was "etherised", or whatever.'

'Past is past, man. We're on a footing now.'

That drew two pairs of eyes down to four sets of toes. And maybe we did have something in common, after all: both of us had dropped our hee-hoes to the stones.

'It's not just her,' he yammered, 'though it seems like she fucked us both over.'

'Speak for yourself, John.'

'OK, Mr Hard Guy. Mr Who Cares. Mr I-Do-the-Dirty-with-the-20-Mill-Club-Every-Week… But dig this: it's *me* she wants: *me* she calls when she's in shit, not you.'

'My phone's out of order.'

'Yuk, yuk.'

I asked: 'Is she in trouble?'

'Yeah. Or maybe. Or who knows with that chick. I'm goin' to get an answer. Which brings us back to you. I'll level, pal. I don't know whether I drove up here to see you, to see San's Mom's place for myself or just to snort this fine pollen up my sinuses. But now I'm here and've found you, so may as well make use of it.'

I was willing to bite and see how far it reeled. 'You're proposing?'

'Stay out of her life, and I'll get San to talk.'

'I'd still like that chat with him, true. But so far being in her life is concerned, I'm not.'

'She can change by the day.'

'Or the hour, or minute. But like I say: whatever she may cook up – and there's not much danger of her groping me here – I'm not in *her* movie. I want my own.'

'OK. You got it.'

'Nice. Yours to give?'

He shook his head, chuckled. 'The old man's boy…' Trying to winch his way out of plastic disaster, he added, 'Do me one more favour? in thanks, say, for me bringing the pizza?'

'What's that, ol' buddy?'

'Tell those guys down at the St Trop cop-shop to ease up on our surf friend. I mean, it wasn't like GBH for him to tweak your tires, was it? They don't get his sense of humour, but you do.'

'Yeah. Merry pranksters. Poor Dewey-boy. Sure.'

It couldn't have happened to a nicer guy, you might say; but somehow I was in no rush to bail out the surfer. They were unlikely to send him to Château d'If, unless they found his prints on something else. Which idea, drifting, bifurcated into memory of recidivist car-thieves at Malibu and a wonder as to whether the cloud above that copse was going to spoil a sun worshipper's idyll...

Things come in threes, they say, but no new Italian vehicle spat stones up the drive. So I leaned back into a vision of what it might have been like for Mazandaran and the actress to settle down as Ozzie and Harriet in the Palisades. It didn't come, quite. It wasn't clear from which side the missile was fired, but mutually assured destruction was there from the start. And *was* it credible that she'd turn to me to put him off, or cover him up? Not really. Something with Liskau had intervened, and whatever that was was key. The factotum knew; Loretta too probably, though being sensible (someone had to resist being a snoop) she may have tried to ignore it. But now Loretta was gone and the facto wanted to find her; so too did 'GL'. Jimmy was the grail they were after. What did that add up to?

I was beginning to think about stirring a stump and taking Mazandaran up on the chance to speak to Rafe at long last when cloud gave way to sun over that copse and I spied something like a glint a kid might flash off a mirror when playing cowboys and Indians. Was someone out there, trying to send a signal? Could it have been *her* camped with Jimmy and the Timer? autism, the familiar? I was halfway to my feet to check it out when I heard stones in the poplars.

Taking a wide circuit, I pretended to be semi-autistic myself, or at least demi-conscious. In this guise, I was re-approaching the recliners when my third guest of the day showed. It was Occitan-tunes man, and he ended my rural idyll.

'Venez avec moi,' he gravelled without invitation to demur.

I already had an idea that this guy was more than a driver for one gangster, or maybe two. I even took some comfort in it. I was out on a limb now, recall, and wanted as few spots on me as poss; besides, the thought that someone in authority was keeping an eye on us was more appealing than it had been when I'd been a silly teenager admiring the hubcap-stealers and rebels-without-a-cause at Easter week in Palm Springs. So I got into his Alfa. Off we sped.

There was no music this time. We had a conversation of sorts, driving through hills to the east:

'La pluie vient?'

'C'est possible. C'est mieux comme ça.'

'Comment?'

'Ça vient de Nord Afrique, la pluie. Apporte le sable, pas l'acide comme la pluie du Nord.'

'Ah bon.'

'Oui.' – The word had a catch to it: Langue-doc rather than -d'oil?

'Vous êtes Marseillaise?' I ventured.

'Niçoise.'

As if that were enough, or just to be contradictory, he shunked in the ersatz Piaf/Delta blues. We listened. Sky turned to grey as the Alfa paid court to elaborate curves; eventually, we dropped down towards a pretty lake, part reservoir, part recreation area. Here, despite a French efficiency of guardrails, an upright Panda had managed to find its way off its piste – back to Monaco, presumably.

It was a sad day for one expat Yankee gal on the make. All that palatial splendour she'd commanded when the boss was away, all that pleasure derived from holding the reins of his power, or appearing to – all now gone like the wind. Someone had fixed her wagon. The near-anorexic body they dragged up from the lake was already *volupté* from bloating. Those pins she had crossed and re-crossed for my benefit…

It didn't bear thinking about.

I hung back as my Niçoise talked with the flics. An ambulance came, the gendarmerie, finally a truck to haul her Fiat off to vehicular inferno. Once he had heard as much of the tale as he wanted, my guy sauntered back to relay a potted version of it. This came as he ferried me home to my perch, which told its own story:

It was brakes evidently – a slow drain of fluid, fatal as she'd careened down the hill. She appeared to have thought in a last calculation that it was better to go for the water on one side than rocks on the other. She had opened her door to get ready to jump, but impact with a rail must have brained her. Drowning was the probable cause of her end. A contusion to the skull made it easy.

'Votre mémoire est bonne?' he asked before letting me off into a pre-storm quietude.

'On espère.'

'Alors, souvenez-vous ça,' he said, holding up his cell-phone for me to read its number. 'D'accord?'

I nodded. He did too, then drove away.

12.

Rain came, reminiscent of London – a slow drizzle amplifying towards drama, then lacking the conviction to carry it out. Should I have been homesick? There was a plane tree or two here, just to remind you of there; a marronier, an occasional oak, some magnolias, acacias and spruce. But then there were fig trees, date palms, Italian cypresses, eucalypti; pampas grass, oleanders, plus species you couldn't name, green and coloured. Out there past an olive grove lay budding vineyards; beyond them coral poppies spread up to blue hills. Did I miss London and my 'normal' life? There, after rain, would come pale skies and grey. Here, once it cleared, would be dazzling clarity: if not Van Gogh exactly, then the geometry of Cézanne. And like Dad, beyond patter, I was mostly a visual guy.

Slogging up to the house, I eyed the copse where I'd caught a glint. Nothing had altered: I'd check it out later, once ground had dried. The water-logged conditions made me uneasy… I didn't hate the factotum; but somebody did, or feared her or found her a nuisance. Such a waste. Why did people like that devise lives like she had? What was the point of being a hanger-on filled with envy and inchoate resentment? A crooked growth of the spirit had warped a rectilinear being, making it twist where it shouldn't, set its sights on ephemera, never become truly real or even unreal enough to be interestingly human. A certain kind of America… Well, I wasn't homesick for it, though I knew it in my bones. What I *was* homesick for I was wondering (this all subliminal, you realize) as I entered the ruin and cut a path through its rubble towards the wing that had managed to survive unburnt.

I was hit by a sensation that someone had got there before me. It came on you like a scent in the damp. The door banging behind me, I heard a rattle, a tinkling, faint, like rats' feet traversing a scatter of glass, up, somewhere to the back. I came to the staircase; the tinkling became a dink-dink, like a child desultorily tapping a pan with spoon. Up I went, the wood creaking, the dink-dink increasing, nonchalant, as if cheeky, almost to attract. Passing the room I had slept in, I approached Alexandra's. It was in there, whatever awaited me now. Swinging the door open, I confronted – the Timer. He was sitting in her bed, feasting from a jar of *Bonne Maman* jam.

'Where you been?' he grunted. 'Need you t' git me down to the coast. Gotta get to my boat.'

Was I supposed just to take this in stride?

'How long have *you* been here?' I demanded.

'Long as you have. More.'

So on that point I'd been half right.

'Where's Loretta, and the boy?' I asked.

'Not here. Not anymore. Not with that crowd you got turnin' up.'

'So it *was* you.'

'What was?'

'Out in that copse, signalling.'

'Nope. Been here.'

'In the house?'

'In, around, over, under, nearby… Old man of the woods.'

He was smug as a spook.

'Did you let the juice out of that poor woman's brakes?' I put.

'Poor woman? Ain't nothing here resembling poverty, unless in the category of fresh meat and veg.'

'Listen, old man –'

'Don't "old man" me. I pulled this thing on you once before an' got no problem doin' it again.'

So out from under the covers came his trusty Luger. Another twist in the timber of Yankee humanity? – I'd had enough of it by now. But he was in charge.

'You got questions?' he asked. 'I'll answer this. Yes we were here, three of us. Kid likes the place. Then you show up. Loretta, precautious, had us out in the trees; that's why you may've seen something. Your buttin' in caused others to show – too many; specially that bitch after them. So they skeedaddled. I stayed.'

'And fixed her wagon?'

'Not sure what you mean, boy.'

I said, 'The woman is dead.'

He went bug-eyed for an instant, then got up, fully dressed – the same clothes he'd been in since the first time I'd seen him, even those big brown Church brogues.

'I don't know about no dead woman.' – He tossed a quilt aside. 'My concern's with a live one, and that crazy fool kid. They got the van; I gotta git back to Villefranche. That's where you come in. Do an old man a favour, or do I steal your scooter 'n do it myself?'

'Where have they gone to?'

'From the look of things, 'f I say the world'll know by sundown.'

He had a point there.

'Gone somewhere safe, or I hope. Leastwise far from here.'

I nodded. 'Earthly paradise once seemed close to this place.'

'Well, it's gotta rain sometime.'

We considered the mud at our feet.

'Was she done bad?' he asked after a pause, less full of himself.

'Who?'

'That skunk of a blackmailing bitch.'

'"Blackmailing"?'

He squinted north country blues. 'I thought you were s'posed to know things. Aren't very good, are you?' – Throwing his gun down, he repeated, 'Let's git! I need my boat. I've had enough adventure for an old man; and I ain't no murderer. I don't need this!'

The fierce thing in his eye faded, till he was just what he said: an old man who'd had too much excitement. He'd found a bed because he was tired, devoured jam because he was as avid for sweets as a six-year-old. Whatever he'd done, bad or good, he'd go to pieces now, you could see. He wanted a lair to lie down in, any safe place to hide; an old bobcat ready to limp into the woods, lick wounds and die.

I had a few choices to make. The first was easy: I led him down, put him on the back of my Vespa and set out putt-putting for the nearest SNCF. The second was trickier: should I buy a phonecard and alert someone to be at Villefranche when he got there? because he *had* been the one who'd tampered with her car surely – 'that skunk of a blackmailing bitch'. So who had she been blackmailing, and how did he know? Was the phrase just his way of summing up a character repellent to him, or speculating on what she *might* have done had she got her claws into real knowledge? But knowledge of what? And why should *he* have cared? Was he just one more Dewey-boy having a go? a sour old man in remission of pranksterish youth, settling scores? 'I'll fix her wagon!' What was she to him? Nurse Ratched to Randall McMurphy? Ms Frigidaire from the Air-Conditioned Nightmare that he hadn't been able to handle in his hot youth and so had let grow in his mind into the demon that had driven him out? Had she become the face of why he could never go home again? why he'd wittered away five decades in a mild foreign port? It wasn't that romantic after all, was it, to be an old man in the rain trying to perform a last decent act for some young folks you liked but didn't even know that well. So was it surprising that his attempt at 'protection', if that's what it was, had been ill-judged to a point of self-damnation?

My thoughts ran and leapt like scurrying rats, turning it over. Arriving at a provisional conclusion, they found nothing sufficient to have him picked up. Who would I've called anyway? the gendarmerie? Occitan man? It seemed more apt now that *he* should've given me his number; but when I punched it into France Télécom outside of Draguignan station, it was less to shop an old man who'd done what he had or he hadn't and who wasn't up to much more, than to explore a further possibility that had struck me...

Mazandaran had friends, even if he had problems. Nor did he seem like a guy just to walk away from a deal in a huff because some obstacle had been put in his path. Nor was he such a small fish in a medium-sized pond that one or two locals didn't want to keep him around to be lured by whatever bait they could toss. One had decided to give him a farewell *soirée* – that's what my phonecall told me. I still had GL duds on, mostly in tact; so, invited or not, I set out.

The address was Ste Maxime, down at the edge of the Golfe. St Tropez glimmered like a pot puffer's mirage on the far side. The house was a sprawl on three levels cut into seawall and rock; a crescent of beach with a jetty allowed launches to pull in to disgorge glitzers too grand or tipsy to fuss with the traffic around Port Grimaud. More prosaic types arrived by terrestrial methods; so my scooter was able to slip in unnoticed between the Masos and Bentleys crammed into a narrow drive between the house and coast road.

It was nearing sunset, the weather breaking. Gazing out through a wall of plate glass, you could watch folks traipse up from a last launch. Sharp-etched blue chased the darkness towards the lighthouse at Cap Camarat – another *beau rivage* here, though a touch middle-class compared to Liskau's over Santa Margherita. The rocks at sea level made it seem low, and the lights of St Tropez – hospital, church, citadel – appeared more distant than they were, as if part of some floating outpost in peril should waters happen to rise.

Might global warming wash this Sodom away? The spectre occurred to nobody present: too much art to ogle, too many sofas to loll on, too gorgeous scenery beyond glass and parapet. Nobody here could think of anything more painful than a shrewd picking of pockets of easy wealth. Everyone seemed to have it, or to pretend to. Not of few hailed from the old country: a bray over hard rock held accents not unlike the one of the gal from whom we would hear nevermore. But fear of mortality lurked in no faces. Eternal confidence exuded from the guffaws, the back-slapping, quip-making, shit-eating grins. I was a wallflower at best in the context. Most would be. To be a fly on a wall may have been preferable, but then I wouldn't have had a chance to note the big man's reaction on spotting me.

This didn't happen, at first. What did is that I recognized one or two of the North Africans serving – same as at Alexandra's, night of the fire. A thought quickened at this, a flare under an idea that had once failed to ignite; but since they seemed not to notice, or even to see me, I let it flicker down into the ash it had died into before. Food, view and pale rosé were in any case too seductive; smiles ebulliating from ladies, despite my mug. So I occupied myself in party as party, not stakeout or whatever Dad might have turned it into. I even felt spirits swell for events like this in the past – nostalgia for a life lived for pleasure, inebriation, sexual promise and so on: all the stuff Mazandaran and Co. seemed to want to bottle and sell.

Where was the harm in it? I was no Wahabi. I wasn't even 'pure', like young San as described – he who I looked for but could not find. No, harm would be elsewhere, if it here at all. Dewey, José – that retinue wasn't visible either, nor my Niçoise… Philippe, the designer, and one or two types from PROIE I made out. Snaking through bodies, I caught bits of their chat, about officials, 'police of police', 're-application'. These referred to Mandazaran's club, I guessed. The *she* who might appear at its Grand Opening when it happened must have been his-and-my-cunt-coz's actress.

'Mais, connais-tu? Elle est enceinte, on dit.'

That *was* news.

'Enfant de qui? Merveilleux! Notre Sammy?'

I was pushed on before an answer could come. Implications chased me through many a hip-grazing and arm-brushing over padded boobs, batting me eventually into the first uncrowded space you could find – a powder room, I thought, though on second take it was clearly an office and not where you were meant to be.

Was *it* where harm hid? On a wall behind a desk hung a map of the region, red stars on it – locales of night spots? An area shaded up to the east of Fayence had pinned next to it the same piece from the *FT* Alexandra had fingered. I scanned it again – 100 hectares, wild landscape, horses, hotel, golf course, finance to evade Code Napoléon, pitfalls of private ownership in France… Yes, this may have been where harm hid. But who did it belong to? some financial advisor? *avocat*? ex-KGB/FSB/McMafia Mr Bigskie Big?

I didn't loiter to sleuth. I was back into the bump-and-grind doing disco with the best of 'em before He or my cunt coz could nab me. It was in this posture, vaguely swinging hips and popping tips to 'YMCA' or whatever, that I was pinned at last by the big guy.

Shame, really. I was just starting to have fun. Despite my occasional Euro-sarkiness, I could see that my countrymen and women still knew a thing or two about gettin' it on. But I was summoned. A frown followed by grin too wide – just what you'd expect.

'Hey, pal… glad to see you! I worried about it the rest of the afternoon. Drove all the way up there an' forgot the whole purpose: to invite you t' the party!'

His hombrés were circling, poised for direction.

'No sweat, man,' I grinned back, as phoney as him. 'I don't hold it against you. Great gig!'

José's pecs flexed as if wired to a nerve in the man's cheek.

'Yeah, I got friends. Glad you do too. Who gave you the word?'

'A big bird told me.'

He nodded abstractly; José tensed to lurch; a hand massaged him back. ''s cool; he's kosher. Come to see San; I, like, promised. So after he's had a nudge an' stroke with these babes, give 'im a car, let him go up to Monte; I'll call ahead. Give him the surfer's.' – José thus restrained, he concluded to me: 'You didn't go down to the cop-shop like I asked. Guess you had other things on yer mind after I left, huh? Nice spot up there – taste.' With that, he and entourage faded.

Me? I buried myself back in the scrum. They were playing 'La Bamba', arms stretched to high heaven, a pack of monkeys clambering for vines to swing on. Well, swing away, I thought, hurling myself in: rattle those hips; swirl till you take off – whooee! Eyes closed. Sweat poured. Raucous cries riffed, part karaoke, part jungle grunt. There was a suggestion of rutting rituals here, some of which would go on before night was done. Prey was spied. Lids flared to pass signals to eyes that would vanish before dawn, never to be gazed into again. You could dematerialize, if you wanted – that was the message. Everyone heard it, at least for a beat. Everyone was an autist now, dreaming of dances beyond the normal forever, like a beach-blonde who revolved towards me, college gal, neither pretty nor plain, but just ripe enough. For some reason as one song merged into another, she was bussing me full on the lips, a bull's eye as if between contrasting cheeks. A surge of something shot up, and we were away, she and I, Mazandarans of this world evaded, Fate and its knot of whatever. Because that's what she was fleeing from, knots that bound her. Off on a dream for a tic, she saw me as the Liberator come to cut through, set her free.

We all dream that dream of escape, don't we? before destiny yanks us back, as in my case José mouthing, 'Parking-lot, pal. Keys.'

'Wait a minute…'

'*Now.*' – A fist on my biceps, rough palm like a vise. The blonde dissolved back into the sea of bodies as if she had never existed, which – apart from this account of it – maybe she never had.

'You *are* a baby, aren't you?' the tough guy countered to my plea that he show me the way.

'I don't want to like get in the wrong car, now do I?'

He didn't appreciate cleverness. A real cop type. Nor was he clever himself, not sufficiently. I asked him to let me get my stuff locked under the seat of my Vespa, and he was big-dicked enough to agree. He must have never expected me to have the *cojones* for what then popped up under his nose – the Timer's Luger.

'Hey, man!' he protested as I demanded *his* keys, not the surfer's. I clicked off the safety: no one inside would hear a shot, as he knew. 'Keys,' I repeated. 'And you get in first. I'll drop you not far – not so far that you won't be able to get back before all the pretty gals've sloped off with their fantasy bonk for the night.'

It was nervy stuff, Dad – more your style than mine. But I managed. And who knows? Maybe the surfer's car hadn't been fixed, but why take a chance? José's lack of struggle suggested he wasn't too bothered about it. So was Mazandaran not such a hard *capo* after all? Or did the Niçoise have a string of these guys working for him as double agents? If so, what loomed behind that? the Sûreté? Liskau? Surely not the *equipe* I had taken the factotum to spook for. That was a too relaxing theory. It almost always is.

Depositing him in a sunflower patch near Le Muy, I made for Villefranche. It was my destination, I knew. I knew also what I'd find there before I reached it. As the Alfa hummed a pert tune, I wished it weren't so; but maybe I shouldn't have. They were better offshore: safer, as the Timer said, in more congenial waters. The real question was whether they'd waited for him before casting away. If so, the van would be stashed round a corner, and I'd locate it.

That was the hope. It turned out to be the case. So I didn't have to go to a capitanerie in the morning, only to get an amiable shrug. In the glove-box was a map, line pencilled on it – to Corsica. How far along that route they would have gone would be up to me to work out. Tucking myself in the back, I slept on it, briefly.

13.

'You found us,' she said. 'I won't pretend I'm unhappy. A little surprised, though.'

'A triumph of naïveté over time and space,' I said, feeling sheepishly proud. It hadn't been easy.

'I know all about that.' – She drew my eyes up to the mast, where Jimmy swung between cables.

He was humming an Ariel tune, carefree as a colt on a meadow. Only here was more like a Mediterranean fjord: nothing but cliffs under muscle-bound shrubs at right angles, 270° of sea and on the horizon a speck of the smack that had delivered me there.

'Won't he fall?'

'Doesn't usually. And you'll dive in if he does.'

'He can't swim?'

'He can scramble. All animals can. Give you time to catch up.'

'You put a lot of faith in me.'

'Haven't you just shown me I should?' – She brought eyes down. 'Anyway, he's not my chief worry.'

They were hazel and grey. A fine cat's fur.

'I got rid of your van,' I said. 'Drove it back to the rental place, in case someone came searching.'

'You kept the map?'

I pointed to my head. 'Burnt.'

She nodded. Smiled almost. I had never seen her smile, I realized: not really. Would she now? Could I make her? Not yet. Before a new word was spoken, up from below came a groan, and she said:

'That's what I mean. My big problem. May need help with it too.'

The sound rose again: *basso* earthly counterpoint to the ethereal babble Jimmy threw at the sky.

'Go down, will you?' she asked, cat's fur moistening. 'I have to pull anchor.' – I cocked my head. 'I'm glad you've found us,' she repeated, 'but our secret's out. Those guys who brought you may be hard as granite, but money and force buy almost anything.'

Nodding, I set off to do as she asked.

In the sleeping compartment beyond his old *salon du thé,* the

Timer lay flat. His Church shoes were on, like the whole outfit that had not left his body since I'd first seen it. He seemed shrivelled compared to then: Gary Cooper in somebody's lost fantasy. Getting to Villefranche and out here had evidently sapped what juice was left in a creaky frame. The north country blues held all the spark remaining.

'You!' he muttered.

'Yeah, me again.'

'I didn't do it!' he grunted and, hawking, 'I didn't do what you said. I only wanted to scare shit outa her – an' am payin' for it.'

The old lids came down.

'I'm sure she earned scaring,' I offered. 'And I doubt brakes were the whole story. That hill down to that lake's not steep; someone may have rammed her from the rear. Same party probably tapped a shellalagh on her skull once she stepped out to mouth off.'

He lifted a lid. 'Think so?'

I had no reason to. But with him on his last legs what good could it do to lash him with an idea that what he had done that he thought was so good had turned out to be recklessly evil?

'Thanks,' he muttered, dropping lids again; and I stepped back wondering if he'd cottoned onto my ruse.

It was hot in there, rancid-sweet, impossible not to want to go. But he wasn't about to let me off easy.

'Your father,' he began after a throat-clearing; 'I knew 'im.' – Eyes lowered, trouble breathing… 'Down here. He came to Cannes. We used to have pastis on the quai.'

I waited. The eyes rose. He was about to tell me more when an engine shunted on, and I could only catch buzzing. That old tub had catarrhs of her own, and by the time I'd put an ear to his cracked lips a cry like a hawk or an osprey had split the air above. Then came a splash and Loretta's voice calling 'Man overboard!' Naturally I was up, out and on deck in a shake.

I wonder now if down below some plank of consciousness an obscure impulse was at work and whatever he knew or intended to say about Dad had always been destined to stay unheard. A woman's cry, a boy's fall – these were what Dad would have wanted me to care about, not some old story, even about *us*. If I were his son, I'd have to forget idle chat about him – that was the message. At least I'd have to give it a rainy day status, a rank in the realm of the serendipitous. So I jumped. Over a rail I went, still in GL mufti, suede loafers and so on. Jimmy was flailing: he'd hit water, not deck or cable, so was unhurt. The head bobbed up grinning, as if such antics were all part of life's grand procession of joys, which maybe they were. Realizing that what seemed like disaster might end as a game, Loretta teased me as I swam for him. He dodged and splashed, determined to have as much fun as he could; she cut the gas and, tub idling, watched me herd him around to the lee, over which she threw a rope. This negotiated and him back on deck, she shouted 'No!' again as he made straight for the mast. Have a thrill once and naturally, being an animal or kid, you go for it twice. As I came up dripping, another 'No!' rang out and, chuckling, he desisted, to go back to circumambulating, whistling his Ariel tune.

Was this for her benefit? mine? both of ours? Who knows what the autist's mind knows or his furtive bouts of glancing can see.

'I think you've bonded,' is what she said as I came up to strip off drenched cashmere. 'He smells something on you... Hang it over there – 'll be dry in a half an hour.'

So I was down to my underpants: GL too, '50s bathing-trunks style; just the thing for a Burt Lancaster who had no call to be modest. Oh well... 'Never mind,' she grinned, pulling the choke. 'We're alone here, or I hope so. Jimmy? Anchor!'

'"Anchor!"' he echoed from somewhere up near the bow and, before droplets could dry on my chest, we were underway again and he hanging over the poop, eying eddies churned by our progress.

I did my equivalent: watched the wild coast recede while catching my middle-aged breath. Thoughts quickened and scattered – Bonaparte's youth, exile and death at my age; the old guy below, Jimmy and my exact place between them. I'd miscalculated before, putting Mazandaran to me as I was to the Timer, which wasn't exact. But why should I have been calculating along these lines then? Did the charts Loretta was studying provoke me? Or were time and immortality just logical toys for the mind to play with in that idyllic space?

'Whe're headed?' I asked her, shaking an ear.

'Corsica's a big island. But if you got here, it's too small for us.'

'You left a trail for me. I didn't find you just by scent. Who else would be so clued in?'

The hazel-and-greys hid behind dark glasses. Mine had sunk to the depths when wrassling the boy.

'Glad to hear you can find your way,' was her response, ''cause I'm going to put you off first chance.' To the blues over her wheel, she added, 'You still have something to do on dry land, don't you?'

'Do I? Maybe. And maybe you could help. Not by coming – it's right to lay low, especially with that old geezer down there. But by helping me figure out all these unknowns.'

She glanced over. 'Only connect? OK, but poke your head down again first, make sure he doesn't need anything. He's had more action in the past days than in a dozen years.'

So I ducked in and, peering round a bulkhead, found him out like a light. Teetering, I gripped onto one of the built-ins holding books about Dad – ancient paperbacks, pages spilling, glue long since dried... Could anyone have wisecracked his way through mayhem *so* chirpily? Engines rumbled; an author adumbrated; I pondered. Then Jimmy arrived, whistling under his breath, and passed me into the cabin, where the Timer's wheezing no longer sounded over a dull racket. He settled at the foot of the bed, draping across the Church shoes, like a familiar pet. Seeing them nestled so cosily, I slipped a paperback back in on its shelf and went topside.

'OK?' she asked.

'Sleeping. Jimmy's there too. Will he wake him?'

'Lullaby him more like. They're tapped into parallel universes, those two.'

So that was alright. But what about me? She glanced over again – chance for conversation? What the old guy had let drop about Dad... she'd said 'only connect'. But my own existential stuff was nothing to bring up: who I was or I wasn't, what I had done or I hadn't, the rebuke of some parent or what was eating me. What was driving *her* out towards that copper-blue horizon was the question. So I asked:

'Why did you split?'

'From where? Alexandra's, or GL's?'

She'd called him Gianni before, GL being the tag of the factotum.

'Aren't they linked?'

'It depends on what you mean by "they" or who. But I guess both were for pretty much the same reason.'

'Her?' I asked, meaning the one no longer with us.

She nodded.

'Is that why the old guy fiddled her Fiat?'

'That was nutty. I tried to stop him, but he's a stubborn cuss. And we had to get.'

I nodded. It made sense. Recalling the scene, I wondered if she, Loretta, had been trying to get to me too – those glints and signals, the Timer as messenger…

'He called her a "blackmailing bitch",' I resumed.

'She'd be capable of it.'

'That isn't exactly a confirmation.'

'I once told you: there may be things best not to ask.' – She turned the wheel windward.

'For you. But if I still "have things left to do on dry land", I need to know what they are.'

When she glanced over, I caught a reflection like in somebody else's lenses. 'What's Alexandra up to?' she asked.

'*She*'s who you're running from?'

'Knowing her motives might help.'

'Her motives for what?'

'Sending the boys to Liskau in the first place.'

'I thought you knew that. You told me – '

'What he told me. What I was happy to think. Not what I wasn't.'

I stared at her, waiting.

'Taking a position that the're things not to ask may mean finding out things you don't want to know.'

'I see,' I said, and did almost.

She looked forward. 'Do you? I'm not sure I do.'

We were at this crossroads when Jimmy wandered back up, content as an earth-spirit, singing vaguely. Loretta's muscles – face, arms – seemed to relax. 'Sleeping still?' she asked.

'Not sleeping, no.' – He wound off on his way, gurgling, and tension surged in her again.

'Take this, will you?' – She handed me the wheel. 'Be right back.' And down she went. And what she would find she would come ask me to confirm. And then it would be up to me to help her:

He had gone soundlessly. Or was the gurgle Jimmy had brought up its parroted sound? With the boy at his feet, he had slept into Forever, adrift in his hearse of a home. Now we had to enshroud him.

The option of port was dismissed. I was passport-less, Loretta on the lam and Jimmy... what would some puzzled, over-conscientious authority make of *him*? We were lawless here; and wasn't it a kind of poetic justice to consign him to the element he'd chosen to be rocked on, or near, for the bulk of his days? 'I'm captain,' she mused; 'guess that makes me the priest.' So she would preside over our makeshift ceremony, once we were out in safe currents.

I tied his sweaty sheet round him and weighted it. Jimmy – was he aware? if so, how much? – was asked to sing. 'Happy Birthday' was his choice, it being the sole tune he knew all the way through. Loretta and I joined in on a second reprise; then the shroud passed over the stern and made its way down slowly, swirling as it sunk, Jimmy murmuring more and more softly, until other thoughts took him and led him off, like the weird waking sleepwalker he was.

'Will you dump the boat?' I asked her once back at the wheel. – It was near sunset now, atmosphere still and immense.

'No. I have papers.'

'Won't they ask where the owner is?'

'I own it... Have for years.'

'But he offered to sell it to me in Cannes harbour.'

'He did that to whoever walked down the quai. It was a precaution, transfer to my name, in case something like this happened. It wouldn't have kept him from selling if he'd wanted a flat on dry land. He kept talking about it, but we knew he would never.'

I reflected. It was easy to imagine and conjure in that space.

'You knew him well?'

'We were close – closer than he was with anyone, I guess. Or who knows, an old hermit like him.'

This seemed to cover up what it almost disclosed.

My mind circled. '*Was* he your father?' I asked.

She said *no*, but with tentativeness to it. 'He *knew* my father,' she added, over a swish of darkening waves. 'Or claimed to.'

'You mean you didn't?'

'Is this comfort after bereavement, or interrogation?'

It was a fair question. So I backed off, though I sensed what was coming and had an unformed idea of what it meant when she added:

'I'm sorry. A sore point – maybe shouldn't be… He was a drifter, my dad – not all his life, but by the time I came along. Over fifty when Mum met him. She was Anglo-French, thirty-something, in Cannes for years, helped with the festival, arrangements – I guess that's how they met. It was a fling. I never blamed him for bailing – I ran from her too. Single mums… Maybe that's why I never became one.'

I was tempted to say that her tense was inexact and that life wasn't over, at least not for some. But just then Jimmy came back, winging down the rails; and it was time for supper… Animal existence – thank god for its relief! So we ate. Then, once finished, he was off again and she and I could return to our ruminations.

They seemed to reduce now, or to expand in the whishing under lit stars. I'd begun to realize who she was – 'only connect' – and why I'd been instinctively drawn. She on the other hand knew little about me; surely not who *my* dad was or what that might imply. Why didn't I say? What made me hug it? Did I feel him again over a shoulder, as some Byronic persona rose and vied for control? But who seduces his sister? It's the oldest taboo. Yet, why should it be? And she was only my half-sister, if that. I hardly knew her: we were adults: she liked me and needed a child; so did I. Or did I? Did *we*? There was Jimmy. There was Rafe too somewhere, potentially more adrift, though on 'dry land'. So where was the goodness in it? What was right? What might Dad have done? But was Dad right? Had he been ever? Look at what *he'd* done and where we were now. And what else – what more out there in the unknown unknown – might he *have* done that we knew fuck-all about?

'Anyway, he's dead,' she continued as if a thread hadn't broken. 'Has been for yonks.'

'Our father?' I said and covered by quoting, "who art in heaven"?' as if it were some throwaway line.

She stood braced at the wheel again, Jimmy below. 'Are you religious,' she asked after a time.

'Not really.'

'Out here it's hard not to be. Hard not to feel something.'

'I feel something,' I quipped, regretting as soon as I had, because when she glanced over, you could see that she felt the same about me as I her, or could have. 'How do you know?' I blurted.

'How do any of us?' – Her tone seemed to swim.

'I mean about *him,* that he's dead.'

She turned to her charts and the sea. 'Guess work. Probability. What people say. My own need.'

'Your own need?'

'For something to be certain.' – Fighting whatever had come up back down under that formidable streak of practicality, she added, 'For now we have to think about you: where I put you on terra firma.'

'What about you?'

'We'll be OK.'

'You sure?'

'Don't patronize me, brother.'

'OK… sister.'

It had no resonance, not that she would acknowledge. Something severe had clicked in: that aspect of Dad that was in her but still undeveloped in me. It was bracing, like cool night air, which is not what we were cruising into.

'What happened at Liskau's?'

'I don't know.' – Her tone clipped.

'Was it sex?'

'Possibly.'

'Did the factotum know?'

'Seems like.'

'Who was she blackmailing?'

'Whoever she could, I guess.'

'Not Liskau, surely.'

'That would have been foolish.'

'The actress?'

'Warmer.'

'Over?'

She didn't answer.

'Jimmy?' I pressed. 'Is that why you – '

'Took him away? Yes!… You don't start that sort of thing with somebody like him. You just don't.'

I waited. She was furious, though controlled.

'They were trying it on, or going to. But you don't fuck with emotions like that. And he has them, believe me. It's like taking advantage of an animal, or incest with a child.'

It was passionate, yet *sotto voce,* so that he couldn't hear. But one word she used drilled into me.

'I get the attraction. I'm human – I'm a woman – I *see*. He *is* an angel! Who wouldn't want to reproduce that.'

'"Reproduce" it?'

That stopped her. Then, after a long study of darkness gathering – 'I don't know. I'm not sure. Go ask Gianni. Tell him you've seen us, but not where. Anyway, by then we'll be nowhere near where I've dropped you. I can't risk it. Can't risk *him*.'

At which point the *he* in question wandered back up, and conversation ended. And within hours she would be taking on fuel and I waiting for a bus to cross the island to where ferries set out for Italy.

14.

Genoa is dirty, different. East coast American cities came to mind – Philadelphia, Baltimore – though Genoa is smaller, immemorially older and grander. The history of the arc of coast from Marseilles to La Spezia rose as a ferry approached: it had had its heart here; Nice had been Genovese, Monaco, the old tower over the port at St Tropez. Andrea Doria, Simon Boccanegra… rivals of Venetian doges had plied the seas here, building their castles on green and granite hills gazing west, to where Columbus and brave natives sailed.

Italy was different, I mused on the train going south. A corridor of suburbs carved into rock seemed meaner than its equivalent on the blue Côte, yet at the same time more glorious; lawless, yet richer in some unexplained way, as if the air itself had a tang of native wine to it

– dark rossos, not Provençal rosés. Italy was that much more southern and eastern, though neither so much as to plunge you into real foreignness, like lands of the Orthodox and Muslim. The spirit of Catholicism seemed more exotic here even, as well as the atheism reacting against it. France was lean, agnostic, contemporary, Bizet; Italy in its stones and its deep, lush, dark foliage murmured Iago's 'Nulla!' along with the heart-splitting 'Salve' of Desdemona. Des-*demon*a: of the demons, sweet victim at prayer. Had the battle between darkness and light, evil and good ever been so obvious in Shakespeare as in that opera of Verdi's? Didn't it almost take Italian pronunciation of a name to waken you to the deeper truths, stranger knowledge of all the mixed, complex substrata we humans exist on?

But such clarity! It struck me on making my way down from Santa Margherita station. Such simplicity as you strolled through a market by the port; such a sure sense of what mattered as the women offered porcini, pecorino, herbs; such a keen undertow of what made life worth living… and the good life worth killing for?

I wound up an antique pathway, counterpart to roads snaking into Belair, though through narrower, dense hills. Crickets rehearsed summer song in the heat, among the fig and olive groves. Rich Lombards were already opening their villas, young grandmothers setting toddlers out onto lawns terraced behind lovingly-hewn borders of stone. It was hard to worry about the pickpockets and housebreakers that plagued day and night here in high season. They seemed a mere urban myth the northerners brought, an inevitable price to pay for an idyll, a price all Italians – as old as civilization itself – knew about and had accepted long before, corruption like sin being as natural as stench from ancient, water-logged drains.

The gate in the wall at the foot of Liskau's estate would be locked, I assumed without trying. You don't get into places like that unannounced, and I wasn't into scaling stones just then – my GL outfit was the worse for wear as it was. Carrying on up to where a road met his driveway, I envisaged some Lancia boy lurking to let me in. Indeed, one of the grey touring-cars was just smoothing down gravel as I came into sight; and either my eyes were dazzled or I saw behind its smoked windows two heads that were familiar.

'What's Alexandra up to?' I asked myself, adding, *if* it was her. If it wasn't, who was it that looked so like her, chatting as if normally to a head that looked like Edward's? Edward, that other of her guests who had stayed, like me, undead… There was Zabiha, of course – why did I not think of her? Was it because I imagined some private interest here, *western* interest, that she might be excluded from? Clearly, if it was them, Giovanni Liskau was not – excluded. On the contrary, he would be at the heart of whatever cabal they were making.

I hesitated, pondering again my concussed pate. Trying to consult Dad, I discovered he'd vanished – passed onto the high seas with Loretta, or into me so fully as to be unfindable now. I was on my own here. So, before the gate closed and Lancia smoothed out of sight, I walked in, CC cameras notwithstanding. Why not? Since the last time, I'd been 'working for' Liskau, no? Didn't that explain why no one popped from behind a box hedge to scare wits out of me?

Insects buzzed over gorgeous growths, extravagant, yet orderly coloured. Down gravel past urns beyond which more Lancias parked, the villa rose small and stately. Pale curtains blew in calm breaths through its french doors; sounds emerged faint on a whirr of midday – piano, voices lilting, three or four, tenor, alto, bass, soprano in descant. I recognized *Petite Messe Solennelle*. What could have been more apt? Could anything be misjudged here, or out of place? Wasn't Giovanni Liskau the quintessence of what my old mama used to mean when she'd breathe her favourite French word *raffiné*?

I strolled in, just like that. I could have been the boy who'd blown away Gianni Versace and no one would have lifted a finger. No one was there, except the singers and pianist – motley troupe, German, practicing evidently. The *Kyrie* broke off as I passed, then re-began. A harmonium joined in, making the sound swell. Breeze carried it on, as if to praise the glories of Rapallo and a hundred kms of coastline to Sestre Levante that grew visible beyond further french doors leading onto a terrace that sunk away ever-so-gently on the far side.

The designer lay on a sculpted recliner. It was one of a pair in forged iron, unlikely to collapse. White and yellow stripes of an umbrella shadowed him, a motif carried on in cushions on which his meagre form stretched. He was dressed all in cream: linen trousers, cashmere pullie, monogrammed slippers – nothing more, except a gold watch, pair of rings, leopard-rimmed sunglasses and casque of baked hair. Did he hear the assassin coming? No: *scented* him.

'Dear man! what a pleasant surprise… You have found them? I hope. Come, sit; tell me. Only make yourself comfortable first. A fresh set of clothes is in the room where you were last. Have a douche.'

'Not yet, thanks.'

'I sense polecat, if you don't mind me saying so.'

'I don't. And don't mind *it*, for now. I have a few things to ask you.'

'And I you… Well, if you must. Perhaps an aroma of coffee and fresh bowl of roses may ease it. Yes, the blend may be tolerable, just.'

He gave an order to a servant who managed to surface and vanish in one motion. Then he repeated: 'You have found them?'

'I've found them.'

'And they are?'

'I don't know.'

'You don't know. But you *have* found them. How is it that there should be the one without the other?'

'Because they left where they left me.'

'And didn't say where they were going.'

'Of course not.'

'Why "of course"?'

'Because they – she – don't want you to know.'

He sighed, audibly. The hills behind Rapallo gleamed emerald and jade. 'My dear man,' he continued, 'that she should take such a view I can understand, irrational though it is. But why she should not tell *you* defies logic. Does she think I'll send you to be impaled by some mameluke in Cairo to gain a confession?'

Coffee came – two cappuccini as if whipped by Hebe – also a bowl of pale roses just breaking out of bud: yellow, mauve and, as desired, softly fragrant. 'I can't speak for her thought patterns,' I said.

'Perhaps not. Nor can I. On the other hand I can say that she's being a fool, and quite dangerously so. It is one thing to want to protect a boy and another to kidnap what is in fact a young man.'

'You consider him kidnapped?'

'I told you: he has no choice – not that he can make properly. That is what it is to be autistic.'

'Can he make choices about sleeping with people?'

Liskau licked foam from the rim of his cup. His pause was not long, only pregnant. 'Jimmy is a young animal. What do you propose? That I lace his porridge with saltpetre?'

'I hadn't thought about it. But what I do think, and Loretta feels passionately, is that he should be protected from exploitation.'

'"Feels passionately"? – I am sure of it. "Exploitation"? – Has she made such an accusation?'

'I don't know. Has she?'

He wiped a moustache from below his splayed nose. 'She left suddenly, entirely *sans explication.*'

'What does that tell you?'

'Nothing. That is my point.'

'It's the opposite of mine. It tells me that a thing happened, or had happened or was about to happen, and that she found out.'

He studied a slipper. 'You are admirable,' he resumed. 'Developing brilliantly, just as Alexandra hoped.'

'Alexandra?'

'Yes. She is here too, by the way; you missed her. They went to Portofino for lunch, Edward and she. This is how dangerous Loretta's rashness is. They have come all this way out of concern. I'm sure they'll be pleased, yet disappointed, *very,* to hear what you say.'

Just then one of the players who'd been rehearsing *La Petite Messe* stepped out to speak a few words in a mix of Italian and German. I, being Anglo-Saxon, could decipher it hardly, but the message appeared to please Liskau, because when he'd turned back it was to say,

'I trust you'll stay until evening? They're giving a concert in town, on that esplanade overlooking the harbour – yes, next to the church. They've asked me to sponsor it, and I am glad to. Often people imagine enterprises like mine care only to cater for the vulgar. But I am Italian. I believe in the ancient and glorious. We have traditions. Germans understand. Culture *is* the identity of Europe.'

'Which you pay for by selling handbags to the Indians and cigarette-lighters to the Chinese.'

'I'm not sure that is quite exact. But in any event, whyever not?'

Why indeed? I was sounding like some sour stage-American: Dad as a cynic or Mazandaran as victim of wicked Euro-chicanery.

'Why Edward?' I asked, to get back to the subject.

Liskau clicked his cup on its saucer and poured an inch of Pellegrino into a glass. 'Com'è?'

'Why Edward? Why has he come? I half understand Alexandra.'

'And why not?'

'Yes but *why*? Jimmy's not his son. He has no interest in him.'

'You are well-informed.'

'Are they lovers?'

'Edward and Jimmy?' He almost laughed. 'Dear man, we may be baroque, but surely that goes too far.'

'Maybe it all does. Maybe Loretta's right. Edward and Jimmy never crossed my mind; why should they yours? It was Edward and Alexandra I was asking about.'

The laugh had been clipped. An after-smile faded as quick as the breath of *la dame aux camélias*. 'The sex lives of the old are of small interest to me. You must ask them.'

'I'll make a note of it. What are then, of interest? The sex lives of the young?'

He grew severe. 'Without question. Always. From earliest times… You Americans, half-Americans even, are such puritans still! Prurient, perverse – disgusting. This digging, this wondering, accusing, demonising – how shameful. How dare you? Have you not dreamed? Has no beautiful boy or goddess ever ravished your body as the sun rose? Why do you pretend? What do you suppress? Can you not grasp that it is why you still produce so little of the genuinely erotic, or aesthetic? I may be old, lecherous, even repulsive to your eyes, but I do have a sense of what mortal beings desire. And to serve *that* and to exploit it are not the same thing.'

I let this flow. Into the intemperance of noontide it passed, until its source had relapsed into silence. The musicians had stopped practising by then, possibly to break for lunch. I myself felt hungry and half inclined to deliquesce into his realm of desire and be pampered. But…

'Does Alexandra know?' I inquired.

'Naturally. We all do. The English are not *wholly* separate from the

European psyche, are they?'

'Does she know about Jimmy?'

'What about him?'

'What you've done with him.'

'Be careful, monsieur. Do you know a thing? And what do you expect? What do you think *she* has expected? that I should send him to some diseased Eritrean whore in the old port of Genova?'

'Did you pimp him to the actress?'

'Ahime! Et tu?'

'Isn't that why the factotum was blackmailing you?'

He rose from his recliner. 'She was not blackmailing *me*... As little sense as she had, she had more than that!' He set off, shuffling monogrammed slippers over copper tiles, under his breath muttering, 'I suggest again, sir: shower and change before lunch. Your conversation draws a stench from these attitudes. I advise you: correct them.'

I did go to the room where I'd been once before. I did shower and change, all the while pondering. A few things were clear now – he hadn't denied them. There'd been some setup between Jimmy and the actress. Why? a boy's beauty and a woman's desire, *mania*, to have a man with no lien over her, which the boy couldn't ever. But how foolish! That was just what she'd put herself into: somebody's chance to have power over her – to blackmail her, which is what the factotum evidently had done. Then Loretta had found out: the facto's work too? The one had run, the other acted, or reacted. Remote control had been triggered – 'won't somebody rid me of this troublesome priest?' – and a body had had to be dragged from a lake.

Death by water. But... could it really have been only the Timer's doing? to get her off the tail of Loretta and the boy? It made a kind of sense. She, the factotum, would have led GL to them, which was exactly what they hadn't wanted just then. But if blackmail were in it, someone else may have had a better motive – the actress, or her protector(s) or other lovers; though not *me*. I'd been a target too, after all: in retrospect that was clear. All of which pointed in one direction – our jilted Great Gatsby, Mazandaran.

I had a flash plain as fact of some bad boy like Dewey chuckling himself silly while bashing the boot of her toy Fiat. I'd raised this spectre to the Timer, mostly as a ruse, to salve his bad conscience before Judgement Day. Now, though, it took on such sense as to seem almost sure to have happened. Only one problem: Dewey had been cooling his heels in the St Tropez cop shop at the time, according to Mazandaran. So could others have done it? José for example, even Occitan man, who had brought me the news?

Where was *he* now? – I pondered further, trying to fit all in place. What *was* his game? What was with all of this double network, including even one of Liskau's Lancia boys? That was what I needed to find out here, among other things. There were truly more answers, more questions, much more to be pinned down. Meanwhile, out the window a Lancia was turning into the drive, bringing Alexandra and Edward back from lunch. This served to remind me of one further matter, for which there had not yet been produced a credible explanation – why *her* house had been torched.

The touring-car pulled up and out she stepped. She was wearing a light fabric, lots of it, loose, breezing like the curtains now going slack at the window where I was standing. The day had turned sultry. As her sandals crunched stone, a dead hand seemed to cross the sky, drawing a cloudbank behind it, high humid haze. Exiting the car beside her, Edward looked hot. He had always radiated a choleric rudeness to match the belligerence of his views; now he looked barely irascible, struggling through gravel, eyebrows knit. Was he tired or worried, sleepy from vino or just suddenly old?

They were the gods in *Das Rheingold*, I mused as they clustered, GL coming out from under a *porte-cochère* to greet them. He too looked faded – they all needed siesta, as did the sky. But before that could happen, they had to have a chat. In any case, he had to tell them a thing or two. And what would that be? about me, the uninvited guest? There could be little doubt, I reckoned, as their eyes hoved towards my window and his lips fluttered inaudibly.

The driver I recognized but could not signal. To do what? eavesdrop? take notes? – Did it do to be paranoid? Edward was glowering: what seemed familiar in that? As for Alexandra: she was as unreadable as Gertrude in *Hamlet*, no sign to encourage a bloke to step from behind an arras. Patting her bag as if a chic Derringer were in it, she caused Edward to reach out to restrain her. Liskau seemed to nod them into conspiratorial silence, and all I could say to myself was: ain't worth sticking around, Dad. Time to git!

They started for my wing; I collected my old clothes, dumped them into the tub, turned on the shower again, locked the door to the bathroom and climbed out the window – this was a loo with a view, natch: GL's domain. Setting off down that wide, elegant terrace, I skirted the arbours of olive and fig and came to the gate I had assumed to be locked. It wasn't. No need to scale a wall then: you could just stroll through like some blithe *galantuomo* off to town for the afternoon. Which is just what I did.

Next to the old port the musicians sat taking pasta and rosso *sous soleil*. One eagerly hailed me – German face, open, friendly... we're on holiday here; come join us, etc. No, but thank you, I grinned – what else to do? – and hurried on to the station without, I hoped, appearing in too much of a rush. A train heading north had just pulled in. Wasting not a second in pondering whether to or not, I stepped up its three stairs and rode it out of there.

15.

By Monaco, rain again. It was only a humid day's drizzle, still enough to dampen pristine cashmere. It worried me briefly. There was no angel to wing me up to Mazandaran's this time; I'd have to manage on my wits and cred. Were middle-aged wet dogs in style that week? Whatever, the doorman at the tower at the east edge of town hardly batted a lash as he passed me through. Nor did the desk man hesitate to phone ahead for me, stating my name, which I gave straight, and inviting me virtually in the next breath to go up.

I was expected, it seems. Was that ominous? Was José waiting, to settle a score? Dewey-boy? two for one? Was it possible that Mazandaran, good as his word, had left an order for Rafe / San to talk with me this time? I had a moment in the lift to nurse paranoia. This was where I'd been etherised after all, or so claimed. Was I likely to find a prodigal's platter laid out on the table?

Doors opened. From the mouth of that cave I could see no more than on my other visit: Dad's bad art, Murano glass, sky-and-sea at the far end. Did a susurrus come from that wing-backed rattan chair? Would a boy stand up, flip his phone shut and approach me to seek counsel, penitent now, like a noviciate with an abbot?

Someone got up there. A figure moved in the gloom… It was Zabiha! What was *she* doing here?

'Darling! Such a surprise. Did you just get in? I arrived yesterday. I had no idea you knew my nephew.'

Scrolling back, I suppose you could dimly recall a moment when Alexandra had said, 'Ask Zabiha.'

Only connect. 'Your "nephew"?'

'Dear Salman, my sister's son. Didn't you know?'

Clearly somebody did. But not me.

'Your face, darling! I'm so sorry. I survived without a scratch. But those others… For days now, weeks, I've done nothing but weep.'

This I believed, looking at her. Her sockets were deep, dark; yet they held a fire at core, a slow burn of defiance.

'Poor Luther. Ever wrong, but inceptor of nothing – going along with the others was all he was capable of. As for those women: they may have been crass, but they did little worse than be obsessed with their genitals, botox – perfect Westerners of their generation. But the boy…' Her tears welled: sorrow, anger, passion. 'Such a waste! A mistake! *Tragedy*! Who can forgive that?'

I guessed she was meaning the young neo-con, though why grief and rage should have gathered around him of all of them had no explanation I could think of.

'Come to the kitchen, darling.' She blew her nose. 'We'll have a cup of tea; you must tell me everything. We have no secrets from one another, do we?'

It was a statement, assumption of intimacy, not a question. There was something of the actress in her too – I'd had hints of it before, though they'd never quite registered. Mazandaran and the actress – only connect? Did these odd linkages make sense? he the son of her sister? Iranian diaspora to L.A.? Lebanese-Iranian nexus?

'I'm staying here now. Dear Salman – so generous! He won't

be back for weeks, and the boy who's house-sitting – you know Alexandra's son? – went to St Tropez just as I came. What for, you may ask. St Tropez of all places – that decadent paradise… But darling, you must tell *all*. What has been happening?'

There was a kind of swirl of breathlessness to her. 'Are you the reason he got to Mazandaran?' I asked.

She hesitated hardly an instant. 'You mean Rafe? Naturally. He came to me, or I saw him, after he left that wretched Italian – the one who uses a fake Russian Jew name. How Alexandra allowed it? But I mustn't go on; she is your friend. Where was the boy to turn? sweet young man, clever. My nephew wanted to do business here – L.A., Cannes, similar allure – but spoke not a word of the language, nor any of the languages he should – it is what has become of our people: the Mid East, so wretched! You Anglo-Saxons, the Israelis… Oh, but I mustn't go on. You see darling, I've just been in Beirut and can't help myself. The destruction! the terrible, criminal tragedy!'

There was too much in this. I tried to keep focus.

'Where did he go exactly?' I wondered.

'Who, darling?'

'Raphael. "San".'

'St Tropez; I told you. Salman is obsessed with nightclubs. I blame America, the West, that frightful *décadence*' – she pronounced it in French fashion. 'I tell him to invest in land: it's the sole thing that lasts. I've lived in England three decades: who are the best people there? Old aristocrats, darling – they're the only civilized hope. The fall of the Shah, King Hussein, Feisal before him, even wretched Farouk – what has *our* region come to since all these republics and gangsters and dictators arrived?… Do you take milk? No? Good. I can't find any.'

The fridge was stocked with Chardonnay, beer – Western decadence. So why, you may ask, had *she* stayed here so long?

'But I mustn't go on.' – She ransacked cupboards. 'No biscuits! how dreadful. Here's sugar; you must have something sweet. Almonds. Take a handful.'

I wanted to ask her… what? many things. But I wanted to get away from her even more. It wasn't that I found her grotesque: the 'body of a sixteen year old' offer wasn't re-made, nor did it more than graze memory in the flutter of motifs that seemed to contradict, or at least spread irony over, what she came out with. It was more that her anguish, if you could believe it, seemed justified yet corrupting at the same time. If you credited it too much, you might begin to slide into some area of real wrong, a place where anything could be rationalized and a cynic's illumination light up truths that deserved, like the mystery of Life itself, to stay in the shade. Out of muddle she groped after certitudes which shrank back into muddle the closer they came.

'So Rafe does business for your nephew here while he's in L.A.?' I asked, trying to get to the essentials.

'Never ask, darling; they do what they do. Unlike his brother, who should have been strangled at birth, he must learn to exist in this world. Salman treats him well, but he will move on once he's ready.'

I didn't touch the 'strangled at birth' line – she came from an Ottoman background is how I rationalized it. Was that too gentle?

'I need to find him,' I put, meaning the other boy.

'He was here when I arrived but, as I say, left almost instantly. He did give me his phone number. Let me see – where did I leave it?'

Within minutes, I was at the station again, trying to decide whether to go on to St Raphaël – too late for a boat – or spend the night in Cannes. Why? nostalgia? There being no reason not to, I opted for his name-place and, when I got there, sauntered into a café I'd spent half a night in not long before. It was early enough still to get an omelette but late enough for a waitress to look at me with faraway eyes. This time I didn't sleep by a seawall. But I did get up before the sound of mo-peds had swelled to a racket and watched the town receding again like virtual reality from a first ferry over the Golfe.

We were into a phase of *ricorso* by now. I didn't go to the scooter shop behind Place des Lices, but to one in a side street where no Dewey would be known. Half-expecting his chicklets to greet me at PROIE, I was pleased to find it deserted – no Alfa in sight. Where would 'San' be? 'He can explain things, if he feels like it.' Things needed explaining – by god, they did. Dad was gone in me still and, without him, this kid seemed essential for no reason I could put a finger on. 'He can explain things, if he feels like it.' But only if he could be found.

126

I circumambulated. Police tape was down, but there was no way in. I thought of hanging around but was too jumpy. I went back to town to check out the café where he'd been with Philippe – not there. Beach? Cinquante-cinq? I scooted out Route des Plages – not a trace.

I was about to give up and go back to the Var when a fracas down Pamplonne caught my eye. A gaggle of nudies had gathered around what seemed like a body stretched at the edge of mild shorebreak. Was it dead or alive seemed the question. Towards them I went.

By this point you may think there was something that drew trouble to me, or that I brought it with me like The Nigger of *The Narcissus*. You may be right, or you may be wrong; or maybe the point has to do with imponderables like Body of Fate, or whatever, which we'll have leave to an afterlife of philosophizing. What matters is that it was Rafe lying there. He was twitching, thank god; not inert.

The nudies turned out to be Dutch, and efficient. 'Overdose,' one muttered, studying his arm. After a phrase or two more in guttural mush, they sprang into action. Throwing on shorts, they got him to a 2CV, en route explaining how they'd spotted him staggering down from Bonne Terrasse, eyes slit and tongue lolling. Mercifully, they knew all about drugs, these guys. To hospital they sped him before anyone more officious could show up and raise an alarm.

I hesitated, wondering whether to follow or to check out the scene on my own. Before a minute had passed, some instinctive gene – was it Dad in me again? – sent feet in the direction of Bonne Terrasse.

Overdose? Raphael? 'San'? Mazandaran himself had said it couldn't be. So what was up here? Who had sent him down the strand in that shape, and from where? – It was early season still, mid-morning. The beach belonged to no one but God and me alone. Rain from Monaco hadn't hit here, but wind was beginning to push something like real waves to the shore. I recalled locals saying how this prefigured bad weather, three days of it. Was that what my bones felt, or shock over what had happened to him?

An idea that he might die chewed at me. Was I to blame? Throwing off GL loafers, I struggled through fine sand, brine spackling the cuffs of my trousers. In the Kon-Tikis and Bora-Boras there was no sign of anything suspicious – no sign of much at all. I trudged on, mindless, obsessive. He'd looked like someone – couldn't say who. A face rose and vanished before it had formed, leaving an imprint like the rind of a dream. Meanwhile my toes dug in, riffling grains, and eyes revolved like an autistic boy's arms, back and forth, here and there, weave, return – to what end?

'You do have a purpose in being here, don't you?' I jolly well did! From somewhere deep inside, I was being driven uphill, onto a *sentier*, past a gate marked *passage interdit,* down a private road, half-gravel, half-pavement, into an enclave of estates, each with its own gated drive and guard dog. Between them ran a right-of-way, once fire road, now overgrown. On either side rose high, canvas-backed fences hung with creepers, vines, hedges, foliage hiding grand gardens within from whoever lurked without and vice versa.

I peered around, glimpsed, though with no idea of what I was looking for, until I spied it. Then I was sure as you are when you see what your subconscious has already shown you. Towards the end of the path, before it reached another gate and sign saying *passage interdit,* close to where char marred the hills stretching on to the lighthouse, because arson had raged here the previous year, killing or stunting hundreds of hectares of umbrella pine, rose another villa. Gracious and pink like the ones I'd just passed, it had blue shutters and a turquoise swimming-pool, encircled by plastic recliners. Between sentinel cypresses dotting its drive, you could just make out one or two blue-black, late-model Alfas, their bird-of-prey grills fierce, their rumps high and shapely. More of them would shortly arrive.

16.

Dealing with police in a civilized foreign country requires three skills: being polite, telling the truth and being ready to wait; or, if you were in a magpie position like me, wait and hope – the old *Count of Monte Cristo* formula.

They caught up with me at the hospital, where I'd gone to see if he would survive. The injection had been of air to the veins; mercifully, he'd been able to rip the line out before enough had got in to snuff him. Details were inexact; nor was he in condition to tell them. As for me, doctors soon wondered how much they should say. When they asked who I was, I blurted 'His father', which naturally made them think I'd want to see cops. This entailed dilemmas, and I can't say I didn't have a *mauvais quart d'heure* before they showed. It got trickier once they had, and ended with a trip to the gendarmerie.

I spoke French, the detective in makeshift English. He was a thick-set crew-cut in a white muscle t-shirt; the room was functional, though no windowless, beat-'em-up cell. We two could chat like 'reasonable guys', he assured me as comrades came and went. Nor did he dismiss what I said as the ravings of a lunatic once I'd explained how I'd used the Dad ruse simply to get information.

I had a few things going for me. First, they knew about Dewey and PROIE and the blown Maso; second, a record of my C2 being fried could be traced with a call. The fire at Alexandra's was verified too; likewise Mazandaran's skip-n-jump to L.A.. Rafe's identity was no problem: he'd had some cards on him, and there was no reason I should have lied about that. That I had no passport might have stirred waters, but this guy was 'relaxed': I had a licence and credit card still, so it was no prelude to a tour of Devil's Island.

More problematic was the factotum. Why hadn't I been in touch with what I knew about her? Indeed, why hadn't I been in touch about most events up till then? Did I have a problem with authority? with the French maybe? Sometimes *Les anglo-saxons* did. Could I not put faith in the System? Why should a person try to stay out in the cold? Was I wanting to be some kind of old-time existentialist? Did I long to stroll through life as if a film? He liked Clint Eastwood, this guy admitted;

and who was that other one? cop on the run in Marseilles? – We could agree on cinematic preferences, it appeared. And shortly I found him smiling on me as if I were an old companion produced by the same tropes with whom he could 'level'.

You know what, Dad? I liked it. Went for it. For the first time in my life, I began to see what you found in those Bernie Ohls types down at old Civic Centre L.A.. Or was I just fantasizing this guy into some Midi version of a PJ op like Maigret? Whatever, it worked, his attitude: his sense that he could *see*, trust, get into the way I was taking the world and so 'on the same team' about it.

It got a notch better too after I asked if I could make a call and he said 'Pourquoi pas?' So I tapped in the number of Occitan man.

This was a risk. I still didn't know if the Alfa guys were an unbroken unit or what. But once my man was on the line and receiver handed over so he could learn where I was and in what kind of mud, guess what? As I'd half-suspected or hoped, he was there in dix minutes; Midi French was spoken; they left the room and after cinq more came back to hand me the keys to *his* Alfa and tell me to go do my best.

'You guys are something,' I said, shaking my head.

'Comment?'

'An old sage once told me that French officialdom really knows what it's up to.'

Occitan frowned: don't blow it with blather, this warned.

'Honi soit qui mal y pense,' shrugged the other; and I exited wondering where I'd heard that before.

Was I to be bait? Were they using the first law of wrestling: let the other guy do the hard moves for you? – I strolled into a parking-lot under roiling clouds pondering if there were another factor at work here and always had been: let the foreigners get on with wrestling over their own stuff, unless and until it impinges.

So what could have impinged? Mazandaran's plans for nightclubs? somebody's scheme for development up in the Var? Yes, but foreign investment brought benefit as much as threat, as each new construction around the roundabouts showed. Which truism argued for a policy of wait, watch and intervene only when prudent, or if you had the goods; also of keeping an eye on us odd birds who flew down here displaying a tendency to perch.

My guess was that these guys knew more about us than we did, though that may have been fantasy too. In an era after God, residual yearning for an all-knowing authority is the flip-side to paranoia, no? – Whatever, they'd blessed me with this sleek vehicle: convenient when you considered the weather. There'd been a clap of thunder; now it was bucketing; and zipping around on a scooter, let alone putting a convalescent kid on its back, might have been too self-abasing even for a penny-ante guy like Mazandaran and Co. wished me to be.

The hospital said two days, so I cruised into town. Checking into a hotel just short of the centre, I laid out in its *chambre de bonne* and watched *pluie* beat the roofs. My window faced east: citadel, church, greenery, coral-brown tiles in between. Wind moaned, thunder banged, big clouds rolled, heavens burst and at last the sun sliced through like a cutlass of God. Cables and masts down in the harbour began to sing, mo-peds and scooters to whine on their way back to the Place des Lices. Old boys stirred stumps in cafés and strolled out to test the ground to determine if it was dry enough to return to their sempi-eternal game of boules.

I was happy. The Alfa was tucked up in pampas grass under plantains; no one knew where I was; the boy was recovering, Loretta and his brother safe, so far as I could say. The police were on my side, apparently; the weird and potentially wicked shenanigans of others could go on, but now I felt that – whatever they'd been about – they'd be harder to pull off: harder than at any time earlier. So I slept, visited the hospital by foot, slept some more, ate and ruminated.

The flics would be onto Dewey, José and whomever from the villa at Bonne Terrasse. Who owned it? They'd find that out too, and what it connected with. They'd interview Rafe as soon as doctors allowed: no one could get to him in the meantime; a plainclothesman was on the door. Where could trouble come from? I didn't know all the whys and wherefores, but the boy could tell me once I'd picked him up. 'He can explain things.' No reason not to now. Or was there?

'Why did you tell them you were my Dad?' he asked once we were in the Alfa and negotiating roundabouts.

It was a reasonable question, for which I had only a glib answer. What lay beneath it might have been what he meant – that I'd had no proper dad of my own.

'Were you there?' he continued.

Was I where? This was not a reasonable, or at least straight, follow-up, though it may have led to further, even final, explanations.

'Where are you taking me now?' he went on, covering his first questions, which was all right with me, since I could hardly respond.

'I thought we might take a spin in the country.'

'You mean Mum's place?'

'OK with you?'

He didn't say. Three-day blow lifting, he stared at the sky, as if a spirit returned to earth from some dark place, hoping for *la vita nuova*.

He was a good kid, I imagined. Not once had I assumed that he could have been at cause in my etherising, or whatever, that day up in Monte. Nor could I imagine why anyone would want to inject death into him, which is what mainlining air to the veins amounted to, not just some teen prank gone awry. I longed to ask details, but you know what? I wasn't a cop, and the priority now seemed to be a comforter – if not Dad exactly, at least a friend.

'I haven't been there in a long time,' is what he said to my neglected question.

'You may be shocked.'

'Sam told me. It's James I'm worried about.'

We swept into the D road towards Plan de la Tour.

'That's like home to him,' he added.

'Seems to be happy at sea.'

He didn't query how I had this knowledge. 'He'll need a home on dry land too,' was the reply. 'She shouldn't sell.'

I turned it over. 'She may want to rebuild.'

'How well do you know her?'

'Not like you. And from a different perspective.'

We continued in silence. I stopped at one of the stands they had by the road there, like Southern Cal in the old days. Buying melon and grapes, lettuce, juice, tomatoes – whatever looked nourishing – I got back in, and we carried on. Seeing that he didn't want to talk,

I shunked in the Occitan disc – 'mah polida' – so he might feel easy about it. Did he notice the care I took? What did he make of it? What, for that matter, did I? This was a boy/young man who'd apparently rumbled Liskau, maybe others too – his mom? Mazandaran? He cared for his lamed brother and kept himself clean, all without much apparent fathering or guidance. It couldn't have been easy. He had competence and promise by others' testimony, as well as the evidence of eyes. So where was the downside? the flaw in his moral compass? shard of unreason in psychology? Was there one?

He watched the land unfold and light grow. It was Sunday morning: fitting when you consider how pristine the world seemed. Like him after whatever pain he'd been in, nature was throwing off gloom. By the time we got to the house, it was gorgeous technicolour – blue hills, red poppies, white bougainvillea, lavender... I had flashes of L.A. as a boy. But *his* inner landscape was what mattered here. As he studied the half-burned place, I tried to assess how it lay.

We stepped out, walked around. His eyes strayed to the copse where I'd once seen a glint. Resting on it, they surveyed the land and the view, the sky in the distance, the house and me again, all in one wise revolution. 'Thanks,' he murmured.

What had I done right?

We stepped in.

'Pictures are missing,' he said. 'Has she sent them to London?'

'I don't know. I noticed a Bonnard gone.'

'Others too.'

The tale of bad blood between Maugham and his daughter came back. Was something like it part of what was happening? war between parent and child over chattels? Did the Code Napoléon come into it? I couldn't ask. I was a guest now, though whose wasn't sure.

We headed back outside, to have our picnic. He ate little, to no surprise, though enough so you needn't worry. This was on the terrace, on a pair of recliners redolent of former visitations. I had an idea, subconscious, though growing less so, that if we waited long enough more would emerge. Did he envisage that too? Whatever, he made no move to budge, not at first. Only after a long, meditative while did he suggest a stroll out towards that copse.

We made a long circuit. I'd never got around to checking out the whole acreage before, I realized – its stands of fruit trees and vineyards up the hill, its flat spaces and culverts from which no view could peer and in which a Loretta and James could have so easily hidden. We found tracks of a vehicle up a dirt path – their van? Rafe said little. Here and there we paused so he could inspect a hole, as if curious to know what vole or other had dug it. Silence fell around his minimal explanations; nor did I ask much. Now and then he would point out a dell or a branch which held childhood importance – a hill James had loved to roll down, a thicket in which they had picked blackberries. Idylls were outlined, yet hardly coloured in. You got an impression that these boys had grown up half wild, few footsteps of parents tracing their paths – perfectly credible when you considered that at least one pair of them would have been shod in the latest of GL heels.

This was unspoken. What would come filled it out. It arrived as we drew back in sight of the house, heat of afternoon ebbing.

A Lancia had pulled up into the drive. On the patio waited a figure that looked from behind as if one of those statues you find in old graveyards, drapery immobile, stone white. As we approached, it grew clear that it was too tall to be Zabiha and too palpable to be a ghost, though it looked ghastly enough as it turned.

She had been weeping. Visibly, she seemed unwell.

'Hello, Mother,' Rafe murmured, without surprise.

'O darling…' She stretched out those hands.

He halted a step from her. I did the same.

'What have you been up to?' he asked with no more accusation than the question implied.

She seemed unable to answer, so he went on:

'It doesn't matter. I already know.'

'You know everything, don't you?'

'Not really. Not yet.'

She dropped arms, appeared shattered. Was she? Did she long to repent something in her past – everything possibly. Why? and to whom? this son? Words stuck in her throat, if they were trying to come. Watching, it struck me that maybe she was struggling for some kind of curse. If so, against whom? God? malign Fate? Or was she just groping towards a species of rationalization?

In the end, what came out seemed like a dodge. 'O why do you hate me so?' – The words echoed.

'I don't hate you, Mother.' – He sounded odd.

'Then why do you treat me as if…' She appeared not to be able to finish the phrase. In fact, she looked scared, which seemed to stir his compassion.

'I never *hated* you. How could I? I'm your son. I've wanted your love. I've never had it, not enough – not like James. But maybe James never had it enough really either. Whatever, I don't cling to the idea. No one can live on resentment without damaging himself, and why should I want to do that?'

She brought her eyes up. 'O I'm so happy with you! so happy you're here! I'm so sorry for what's happened. I want you to know it's had nothing to do with me.'

'What hasn't, Mother?'

She looked away, dried a tear. I was put in mind of an old sepia photo of Eleanora Duse. So was yet one more female in this going to hide her motives behind masks of playing actress?

'What's "had nothing to do with" you?'

'What's happened to you?' she murmured, reminding of how the Duse's appeal had been based on over-the-top gestures.

'What's happened to *me*?'

They stared at each other. She was crushed, the look said. She would have to let it drop, any further attempt at explanation. As if to underline which, she fluttered her drapery down on a recliner.

Rafe was trembling – from where I stood you could feel the vibrations – but, though exhausted too, he stayed upright. 'Will you tell me? Won't you explain for once and for all how it happened?'

'Darling…' The word trailed away into the tragic.

'Don't you think we deserve to know?'

'"We"?' – This might have sounded scornful if there had been any force behind it.

'James and me.'

'"Need to know"? James needs to live, that is all. *He* doesn't care. *He* wouldn't torment me.'

It was destined to be circular, this exchange between them. Both glanced to me as if witness, or judge. Each shrugged subliminally. An impasse had been reached, some blockage arrived at many times before. Maybe it was different this time, more having happened, to him, to her, to where they had lived and how they might carry on, together or apart, here or wherever. A great knot of history seemed to be wound up between them. Who could cut it, her look asked. But did it need to be cut?

Here was one question, unspoken. It seemed to merge into a hope that Rafe might let the thing drop, all that was knotted up there. And maybe he would have, given a chance. But now Edward, who'd been in the house through the foregoing – hadn't he tracked every word? – stepped into the middle of it.

'Ah. So... the prodigal returns.'

It sounded all-knowing. Edward had always sounded all-knowing and contrived to be. As if to warn against that now, Alexandra shot a look at him. But he continued:

'Spot of bother, m' boy? Well, you'll shake it off, what? Good man. Well done. Worse in my day. Imagine if you'd been one of those Jews during the last war.'

I always had disliked this crude individual, but now he was simply too much. I stepped in front of him: 'I don't know what you're doing here. Why not stay out of it?'

He considered me; smirked. The red face and hair glowed – booze, doubtless. 'You!' he grunted, insouciant, cheerful. 'What, pretending to be Dad's son at last? Well done. B+, I'd give; though really, why bother? We knew him – oh yes. Had his five days in Blighty now and then pathetic. Used to ring up Alexandra, didn't he, dear? two/three in the morning, blithering drunk. Washed up. Amazing the cult they built round him; but that would be the film people, publicists, what nowdays they call "spin". Need a hero always. Fact is, he was never as clever as they made out – I shouldn't worry: probably not even as clever as you, old cock. Gumshoe with a year or two of fame and some patter, that's all. Couldn't handle marriage. Couldn't mix with people like us. Couldn't face being a father. Couldn't – '

My fists had clenched. One shot out and decked him.

Edward was a big man, but seventy if a day. Reeling back, he bit his tongue before catching his balance.

Alexandra moved not a muscle. Rafe only stared.

'That's another thing,' he managed, spatting a tooth. 'He was violent. Thug really. "Where intelligence fails, send a man through the door with a gun" – that was the line, wasn't it?'

At this he grabbed Alexandra's bag from the table where she'd lain it and, flipping its fabric inside-out, produced a Beretta.

'Edward!' she murmured.

'I told you,' he growled, spitting crimson, 'you were a fool to involve him. What on earth was the point?'

She stared at me. It was cold, neutral, but not hostile.

'He's brought my son back.'

'Brought him maybe, but not back to *you*. Ask him.'

Her eyes moved to Rafe. They were glazed: was she drugged? I recalled Claus von Bülow, who had hung around their scene in the 1980s, after that scandal in Newport re his heiress wife's overdose. Was there some analogy? Edward and Alexandra weren't married. What *did* he have to gain here?

'Go on, ask him,' he went on, nodding at the boy.

'Ask him what?' I intervened. 'I'd like to ask *you* what the hell you think this has to do with you?'

Edward chuckled.

Alexandra muttered, 'Put the gun down, please.'

Rafe touched my arm to inch me away. 'I know everything mostly, like she says. You have a right to know too. Tell him, Mother.' – He turned to her. 'I'd like him to hear it from your lips.'

She gazed at, or through him, eyes receding, glaze increasing. Immobility had become almost absolute in her, as if she *were* that statue I'd imagined at first. Meanwhile, the doors to the Lancia out in the poplars opened, first the driver's, then by his hand the passenger's; and out towards us stepped Giovanni Liskau.

Hearing the sound, Edward had glanced back. On the chance, I leaned forward and twisted his hand, the one holding the gun. It dropped, hit the stones, fired. Rafe snatched it up and, emptying cartridges, hurled it into the charred remains of the house.

Liskau approached. The Lancia guy hung back. Again, it was one of the ones who had driven me.

'Edward!' purred the designer. 'Such melodrama! but we are not rehearsing *La Forza de Destino*. You always fail in the seductive approach; professional deformity perhaps. I admit there is a certain blunt masculinity in your manner which some find attractive' – an eye to Alexandra, who stayed inert. 'But it is no way to cajole or to caress. I'm afraid you are unlikely to convince those we confront by it.'

Edward pulled a grimace. It made you half wonder what had gone on between these two years before. For his part, Liskau held out a handkerchief – silk, luminous pearl. Grasping it, the other came down heavy on a recliner beside Alexandra's and mopped his mouth.

'Shame for you to turn it purple,' Liskau mused. 'But then, Jacobean colours may be more chic than this brute *noir* you have in mind.' Turning to Rafe and me, he continued: 'I will tell you the truth now; judge as you will. Both of you have run from me as puritans; neither quite understood. Perhaps it's because neither of you ever had proper fathers, yours a stand-in' – to me – 'yours a fake' – to the boy.

'Take care,' Edward hissed. 'You may tear the whole fabric.'

'My dear,' quipped the other, 'I am an Italian. We were creating dynasties when your people were running through forests in woad. We were wearing purple dyed not in blood but in extract of flowers and earth; herbs pressed, refined and distilled. This is the point you fail to make for these boys – you are too much of a Celt for it. The world is a realm we are lent to beautify, if we are able; that is our choice here, our mission – pleasure, enjoyment and glory, or miserable descent into resentment, war, hunger, grief, self-denial et cetera. I come from Naples, not a London suburb like you. I know the inferno; you only wreak it by remote control, with your bombs and mania for Anglo-directed world domination. Very well. I'm no political man; you may do as you like. Only leave me the opportunity to plant civilization after – to bring decoration and joy in your wake… That is my preamble.'

Returning to us, he put on a mask of regret, the man being no inconsiderable actor himself:

'It was the 1980s. We were nearing forty, pretending to be thirty and remembering what it was like to be twenty, amid *fêtes galantes*. After the War even you English had hardship, rationing. In days when we Italians were reviving – *L'Avventura, La Dolce Vita* – you still had your Cecil Beatons, Edith Sitwells. Then came the '60s. You, Alexandra – so pale, so tall, so remarkably thin, well… we knew one another. We were making our way then – the drugs, music, fashion… Then came '70s gloom. When it began to lift in the '80s – Mrs Thatcher, your actor-President over there, the defeat of the Red Brigades and generals in Argentina – we had a last fling. Remember? It was at the house in Holland Park. Edward, your wealthy wife was away at her family place in Wiltshire, and you and I and your *ami* Luther, not yet crippled, and Alexandra – your husband who knows where and with whom – and your Pre-Raphaelite "girls" – '

'Stop,' she murmured, as if he were going to slander the dead.

'You'll tear the whole fabric,' Edward repeated.

But Rafe said, 'Go on, please. We have to hear.'

'Of course you do,' agreed Liskau. 'What's more, you have to not run this time. You have to learn.'

'And forgive?' breathed his mother.

To which Edward scoffed. But Liskau, ignoring him, asked rhetorically: 'What is evil? Not pleasure. Not *life* – I can never believe that… We were young still, if only just. We had our needs, our desires; so do you, if you will only admit to them. Running from my house was childish. When a person finds you attractive, male or female, be flattered: you need not bend – you have choice. As for your brother's choices…' He turned to me: 'In all fairness he must have some. Denied by fate as he is, to take *that* away would be truly heartless.'

By now Alexandra had shut her eyes. Rafe was studying her reactions – was it why she hid them? As if unaware of any implication, Liskau continued towards her,

'We had a party – recall? You powdered your hair like Marie Antoinette, the others too. It was Carneval – Venice, Rio. Vivaldi was playing or perhaps it was samba, or both. You three started to cavort through the house barefoot, waving your crinolines, and you, Edward, in full 18th century libertine mode – it was a time of vogue for Casanova again; the New Romanticism, I think they called it; dreary feminism in any event paused, and socialist chic... Who can describe *exactly* what went on then? Edward, you gave chase. Naturally Luther did too: he always paid you the compliment of strictest imitation. The girls were keen to get everyone at it – there were puritans there too; always are. I would never resist such excitements, but not a soul was concerned about me, except as *voyeur*. You, Edward, determined as ever to play dominant male, ran down and subdued the clearly dominant female; Luther did what he could with the rest. There were disappearances, cries, flitting of nymphs and satyrs in baccanale, suggestive moanings. But not everyone could join in the spirit – why is it they never can? *That* woman; *your* father; Alexandra, even you... What happened? Tell us precisely how it went so wrong?'

But her eyes remained shut. Was she trying to dream her way out of this pre-history? Rafe took a step towards her, touched a shoulder. She slumped into his arms then, as if she too were now of the dead.

17.

I remember imagining absurdly that the gun when it went off had sent a bullet into the voluminous folds around her. Impassivity and pain had been so established in her by then that a shot through a lung might have been just one more thing, and no reason to cry out. But as she keeled over, there was no blood on the fabric. Her pallor was so grey that she could have been stone, if not for the suppleness, weight and residue of breath gurgling. Jimmy's sound on the boat when the Timer had copped it came back as, with Rafe, I jumped into action.

Edward and Liskau faded away as we transported her to the Alfa. The Lancia guy insisted we let him drive, and before you could say boo to a spook, she was in hospital being attended to by the same attractive Senegalese I had awakened to find gazing into my magpie features the day after the fire. Rafe stayed in there with her. After twenty-four hours we learned she would live. Septicaemia was diagnosed. How long she had had it and how she had contracted it were mysteries.

There were many things that would remain mysteries now, and others that would be nudged towards resolution. Dewey, José and Co. had been picked up by the flics, the villa at Bonne Terrasse identified as a rental in the name of the designer Philippe. Re injection of air into the boy's veins, investigation was still going on. It appeared that, like me in Monaco, Rafe had been etherised first, then laid out as a post-teen druggie rather than middle-aged drunk – credible enough for where they had dumped him, whoever *they* were.

The why and why then? We could speculate, or I would, along with the detective. Rafe for his part remained *stumm*. Did he want to forget, or was he preoccupied with his mom? – She came around, and I spent half a night with her so that he could go sleep in my *chambre à bonne*. This was crucial. It was the moment when she chose to level with me, or appear to, making me swear secrecy first:

'There's an end to the story Giovanni didn't tell, though he worked it out years ago. Actually, I told him – trusted him, oddly, rather like you... It was rape, effectively. Edward – he so lacks finesse. As for poor Luther... he did the same, though not with me. *She*, the one he had, got away somehow – out the back, before your father came. Your father... he *was* a hero, after his fashion: I have no doubt Edward recalls more than he let on when you biffed him, which is just what *he* might've done, and more. Luther fled like a frightened hare; he'd have his come-uppance – the stroke not long after. What ended the evening was your dear papa getting me out of that Bosch painting and home to a pitch-black house. The boys' father – I'll always call him that, whatever the truth – was off somewhere. He comforted me.'

'"He"?'

'Your father.'

She glanced at me briefly, then shut her eyes. A nurse walked in maybe; Alexandra said no more. Before I left though, she re-raised lids and, gazing far off, concluded: 'There's DNA, if you must; though, as Edward says, you may tear the whole fabric.'

For whom? And what fabric exactly?

Liskau was back in Monaco by this stage. Edward had high-tailed to London, evading detective questions. Maybe they wouldn't have been put to him – I had an idea of how those guys worked now – but he couldn't have known that. In any event, he didn't stick around to risk it, nor to invigilate Alexandra's condition, which told its own story, though not a lot about what was still unknown. This I would have liked to chew over with Rafe – *his* son? my half-brother? But you know what? Again it seemed too delicate to touch, and he had receded behind that poker-face. Who was I to tell him to drop it?

These are the facts; nor would *I* share all of them with the dicks. Alexandra had almost died; so had one of her sons. The latter had been intended – what of the former? Suppose it had been intended too: where was the link? If she had been poisoned and Rafe were gone, who would have profited? Did it all have to do with the house? with the land? Did the original arson? Sale and / or development could have been blocked by her, Rafe or both as heirs to her husband, who remained the boys' legal father whatever DNA said. That left James, who could have had no say of his own, clearly. But he would have been full heir if the others were out of the way.

Cui bono? Whoever controlled him. And who might that be? Loretta ostensibly, but she had no legal status; and how likely was it that *she* would knock off the boy's mother and brother, let alone have a chance? Liskau held a better claim, as the boy's guardian: James had been sent to him – Loretta was only minder via his choice. But why would someone of Liskau's profile have wanted to stoop to such crime? What could an international mogul need with land development in the Var, even a glittering new town named for him? Of course I could ask – and would. His tale *had* been cut short by Alexandra's collapse. In addition, there was a third possibility – Edward's interest – which he alone had the cunning to rumble:

The Alfa having gone back to my mentor and scooter to the rental-shop, I travelled to the Rock for what I supposed a last time by my favourite conveyance – ferry over the Golfe. Ah, the exaltation of it! The light and the air... At St Raphaël, I made my way up to the *gare*, longing to stop for lunch. But nostalgia belongs to events that can't be repeated. So I evaded a waitress on the far side of the Place, kept to my piste and soon was eying the red towers of Esterel and deep into study of horizons as distant as Monte Cristo.

God knows what you think of in such gorgeous locales, even when strapped to all-too-worldly concerns. I can't tell you a bit of what crowded my mind then, evaporating like dew as Cannes and Nice passed. Does it matter? Doesn't most of the best in existence fade like dawn glow, leaving only sensation, inarticulation and mood? Can anyone describe what he's longed for most intensely? Could Dad? Would you even want to press it into words?

This is what Liskau told me, in essence: 'Your behaviour, dear man, if you don't mind me saying so, is permeated with wish-fulfilment. You must recognize that, and the distortions it causes, as you weigh up theories. What I've been trying to say to you – and it applies to Alexandra's boy too, and Loretta – is that to react in this puritan manner may provoke more damage than it seeks to prevent.'

He had led me out to sit where the factotum and I had sat once and I on my own once before. That terrace facing west, impressionistically dappled by leaves, could not have been said to have had a view worse than the finest on Earth. It was imperceptibly clearer and cleaner than at Santa Margherita. And maybe because it was *his*, not *Maman's*, the place made Liskau seem surer, healthier and as efficient as he had appeared the first time I had laid an eye on him.

'Your father,' he continued in a silken purr, 'made an error, I've always believed. Why he came to that party we'll never know. What was the attraction for him of people like that? I meditate on it sometimes. What makes a terrorist go to a porn film before driving a plane into a tower? What makes a girl who'll end up in nun's habit read magazines advertising undergarments we design for Russian gangsters' molls? It's all part of the eternal mystery. As for your father, to get back to it: why, when he saw where that party was headed, didn't he simply stand up and leave? Why did he linger – even, you may say, "mix in"? Why have *you* mixed in here? You have little more than burnt bones and a scorched cheek to show for it. Is it as simple as that Alexandra asked you? But asked you for what? to meddle? to nose something out? to peer under toadstools? Or did she simply want you to locate her boys in order to tell them civilly, neutral as you seemed, that their father's house had been the target of a criminal arson?'

'Is that what it was?'

'Isn't that what the police told the papers?'

'Don't you believe everything you read?'

'Why should they lie?'

'I'm not saying they did. But police sometimes tend to give explanations when they're not sure. And often an unsure tale put out as fact induces a sense of closure to make the real criminals careless.'

He stared at me. I waited.

'You are a recidivist, aren't you? just like your father. You feel compelled play hero, no?'

'Mustn't someone?'

He continued to stare... the ferret features. At length they began to spread into a grin. 'Perhaps. In any case it is inevitable that fools may rush in, and that fools may sometimes be angels.'

I tipped my hat, figuratively.

'So,' he concluded: 'what is your theory?'

I told him – that is, narrated a version of events in which, Alexandra and Rafe being dead, Edward stepped forth as guardian of James, based on DNA tests, and claimed the land in the Var and sold it for deca-millions.

Liskau emitted a chuckle. He contemplated a shoe. 'My dear man – dear *boy*, I think I must say – you are clever. Ha! I agree that Edward is capable of much, but poisoning Alexandra? And even if you posit that, how did he manage the murder of Rafe via those cretins who tried it? Does he have some link to them? I'd be willing to wager half the shares in my empire that you'd find none. As to paternity of Jimmy: again it is possible, and perhaps a fine joke, that a man of Edward's proud intelligence should father an autist. But what of the brother? Could he truly be such a monster as to kill his own blood simply because the child has a mind of his own and opposes his wretched schemes? My dear, *you* would make a fine Florentine out of the era of Machiavelli.'

I could see that I knew something he didn't or, as per Alexandra's hint, he *did* but chose to appear not to. Why? Out of deference to her?

'What if the boys had different fathers?' I put.

His gaze scuttled inwards. When it came back, it was onto my face, which he searched carefully. 'There *was* a word in one of his plays – their real, or perhaps *un*real, father's... "Polyphiloprogenitive", I think it was. The satirists made a meal of it.'

I waited. He offered no more.

144

'Shall we take lunch now?'

I shrugged.

'Here or inside?' he wondered, then answered himself by adding, 'Inside, I think. It is June now: too hot by mid-afternoon…' Summoning a servant, he rose and, gesturing me in towards a guest bathroom, retreated elsewhere, trailing, 'I go for a wash.'

There had been no remark about my odour this time, though my trek to the top of the Rock had been no less arduous than up a stone path in Italy days before. Did he feel it no longer wise or needful to twit me, or was it enough to instruct a servant to knock on my door as I finished my ablutions and, once I'd cracked it, hand through a fresh set of clothes? GL was not a famed host for nothing; and when I came back out, freshened, it would be to a table set simply yet elegantly just inside the french doors. It would also be armed with new knowledge – had he meant me to see? The Bonnard missing from Alexandra's villa was hung in the corridor I'd been obliged to pass through.

'Much better,' he muttered, adjusting the tails of my shirt. 'It is worn thus, not stuffed in the trousers *comme ça*.' – Rearrangements allowed him to attempt what he had never before. 'This way we needn't speculate on what may have distracted a certain actress…'

I sat. Apparently there were more possibilities to jug with before our subtle dance *à deux* had swirled to its end. But I had a new source of impatience. 'Tell me about the Bonnard,' I said.

Surprise is an old weapon. Gianni Liskau, however, was an old combatant: he hardly blinked.

'Bonnard?' – The servant poured rosé, very pale, hue of flesh in the painting. 'Yes, I see what you mean. Why I should have it, especially since the *femme à bain* it depicts is so far from my type? But Alexandra *is* fond of it – "She has the body of a sixteen year old, don't you agree?" In fact, the one depicted is the painter's wife.'

Taking a sip, I worked to place an echo.

'She gave it me,' he went on, imperturbably.

'For safekeeping?'

'You must ask her, though she may have forgotten – she's having a dreadful time, poor dear.'

The servant returned. She was North African. Did she recognize me? No sign was made as she served a cold soup.

'My concession to English cuisine,' he murmured, lifting a spoon. 'It is the one thing they do well – as the French say, "cold soup and warm beer".'

'I'll pass on the latter.'

'I too.'

We swallowed. For such an elegant individual he made a gross slurping sound. 'Why you?' I inquired.

'Why me which?'

'The painting. For safekeeping.'

'And why not? I told you: women trust me – they have no reason not to. I ask nothing of their bodies, but to beautify them.'

'You also said you and she were once lovers.'

'Did I? How indiscreet. I must've been very young and she very insistent.' – More slurping.

'Who took it?' I wondered.

'What, her virginity?'

'No, the picture, though it's fascinating you should think that that's what I meant.'

'Girls find it a burden they wish to be rid of; but with a kind soul, not some rapacious monster.' – He was evading my question and knew it. 'My secretary took it,' he conceded at last, putting his spoon down; 'also some other items, from her villa. You know who I mean – the one whom we must say drowned.'

'I thought she was up to no good. Why?'

'Ach, these questions! Why did she drown? You know the answer. How did it happen?'

'No why she took the picture and "other items"?'

Wiping his lips, he slipped his napkin into a ring. 'Are you suggesting things of such value ought to be left for mice and thieves?'

'No, only that she knew or you knew, or all of you did, that the next step was going to be demolition.'

He stared. His metabolism seemed to register a subtle blip, as if soup had gone down the wrong way.

'One of my theories,' I went on, seeing no reason not to, 'is that

146

you did it.'

'I? did what?'

'All of it. Torched the house – not you, but whoever you hired – to get her, Alexandra, to sell. You sent me to find Rafe to fix it so that he wouldn't squeak. You tried to get leverage over James too, also using me, to fix his choices. The factotum was in on it possibly, probably. But she became unreliable – too knowledgeable doubtless – so a problem.'

His face was as impassive as a Minoan statue's. 'Continue,' it said. 'Or do you wish me to answer?'

'I'm just fishing.'

The servant removed plates. Could she have been one from the night of the fire? farewell bash for Mazandaran?

'Your theory is full of holes,' Liskau explained, slipping his napkin back out of its ring.

'Work in progress. Your autumn collection may need last a stitch or two, too.'

'And will get them. And will make my shareholders many more millions. Which brings us to a point that you with *your* mind might have already grasped: why would a person like me wish to engage in a charade such as you describe? to build some development up in the dirt? Honestly, sir! I am a Neapolitan, not a farmer.'

Crayfish salad arrived. Neither of us looked at it.

I said: 'Are you? I don't know what you are, really. Even your name is false, or somebody thinks so. You said you had lied all your life – why stop now? we're not in a contract together. And maybe you *do* want part of a real estate pyramid scheme. Maybe you need it for your "shareholders", backers, whatever gang from Campania or money-boys from Moscow finance you. How do I know you're not a secret bankrupt? It's not a message you print on a t-shirt. How do I know you're not a "Florentine from the age of Machiavelli" yourself? in the game for the game; no law, no morality, only "culture"? Even Nero had that, "sir". Adolph aspired to it too – a German.'

'Austrian,' he corrected.

'Closer to Italian. My point is: it never stopped megalomania.'

He smirked. 'You are finished? Shall we try a dish?'

I would have loved to. It looked delicious. But my intemperance had chased my hunger.

'Supposing,' he went on, savouring a bite, 'that what you say is true, I would ask you back simply: who tried to kill *you* two times, and why? Was it me? some "thug" you imagine I hire? But what for? the pleasure of strewing corpses over the Var? And that fire: why is it you have not asked yourself who else was present that night? Why have you not asked *me* to tell you more: for example, the end of the story Alexandra so opportunely cut short? Has it not occurred to you that someone else may have had motives and that that someone may be the same one behind other mysteries?'

I was getting a message, yet still at a distance.

'Has it not occurred to you that that someone may be a person Alexandra wishes to protect, out of misplaced pity perhaps? guilt over Sapphic desire? My boy, I know things you puritans, dabblers in the erotic life of the soul, can only guess. Why did I take the Bonnard? Why did *she* take it? Why did Alexandra cherish it so? *Cherchez la femme*, monsieur. You have another visit to make, surely. Would you like me to have one of my men drive you?'

'No,' I said chastened, and not a little bemused.

'Whyever not? Who on earth do you think has been looking over you up till now?'

'I don't need your protection.'

'Don't be boyish. Do grow up finally.'

'Thank you for lunch,' I concluded, 'and the clothes.' – I was out of my seat and halfway to the door when he called to my back:

'You still haven't found *them* for me as you promised. Or do you not consider that a "contract" either?'

18.

Past the castle and cannons and statue of a 12th century Grimaldi as hooded monk, down the battlements over the harbour, through La Condamine, up the scalier below the Hermitage, out by Café de Paris... Jumping on a municipal bus, I was at reception in the last high-rise in the principality in five minutes. I went up in the lift, but – she was no longer there. No surprise. Where had she gone? Not a clue –

no surprise either. A breath of a thought sent me back towards the station – wouldn't she have made for the airport? But then what? back to Beirut? If she'd wanted to stay there, why she would she have returned here? What other options did have she? back to London? Soon possibly: she *had* lived there thirty years, after all. Back to the 'scene of the crime'? of the crime*s*? Where was that exactly?

I got on TER again, heading west. With no Alfa or Vespa, I couldn't get up to the Var; but I didn't see her going that direction. The question of what she knew and via whom was perplexing. Could she, for example, have shown up at Alexandra's hospital bed? Did she know of the poisoning? Had she been responsible for it? If so, why? – I tried to reserve questions, not jump to conclusions. This was a Muslim woman, remember: I didn't want to be categorical, didn't want to blame *them*. Still things had happened, and she'd had a place in them: a place she'd kept secret. Wasn't that sinister?

St Raphaël. Arriving too late for a last boat, I glanced towards the Place and the café; then hopped a bus. It was packed, being mid-June – *tout commence*. With high season now only a week away, traffic was thickening around the bird sanctuary, St Aygulf. Blue hills floated out there like paintings, growing paler the further you gazed... Ah, this place! such colour! such transcendental intimations! such nostalgia-drenched vistas of vistas, memories of memories – though of what? the Chouf mountains? Caucasus north of Tehran? Tehachapis and so on rimming old L.A.? Was it just the scent of some eternal Elsewhere you felt? a yearning for that Better Place always more fantastic than your own? more beautiful even than *this* in hot rush hour, stuck in a carrefour around Ste Maxime?

Port Grimaud came; the D-road to Plan de la Tour; roundabouts in the gloaming – La Garde Freinet, Le Croix Valmer... Up to Grimaud, where Christmas-y lights swung over the *trottoir*; back down the same road – Gassin, La Foux... I realized that the next roundabout held that spoke veering off towards the new shopping-centre. Up I went to the driver and asked to get down.

Sooner or later you are driven by instinct. Sooner or later it has to be relied on, or not. Hadn't I learned that by now, Dad? Or had I just come to a stage of letting it all go, like you apparently did after running out on me and Mom, and Loretta and *her* mom, into booze and an orgy in Holland Park?

What a tale! Could I believe it? If so, weren't we all weirdly linked? scrapping together in one extended, dysfunctional family? If so, so be it. But where did Zabiha fit in, let alone her supposed nephew, big would-be bossman Mazandaran?

I approached the building on foot. It was dark – a big blockish sepulchre. No one was there, not an Alfa in sight – *nada, niente*. The other establishments, stone-dead. Why was I here? Slipping around in the foliage, I could find no way inside. How to crack it? Who would know? Mr Occitan-tunes? Rafe?

I needed a mobile. Days of fusty, antediluvian lecturing were a lifetime past now; still, I hadn't come into the contemporary world. I *did* have a phonecard in the wallet somewhere, and France Télécom *did* still cater for us tech-averse wretches. A pair of callboxes were in sight, lit up even, down in the mid-centre.

Who to ring? Was Occitan really a pal to the end? Was it possible he might reel in the line before I'd caught the last fish, or the world might turn upside down and angels become demons? Who do you trust? Who do you want to be trusted by most? In other words, who was I willing to call then and potentially be betrayed by?

Next to my phonecard was the number of Rafe's mobile, which Zabiha had given me: the number I'd neglected to dial on the night when I'd chased a phantom in St Raphaël. Now I dialled.

'They got your phone back for you?' I said when he picked up.

'Who?' he wondered.

'The flics.'

'I never lost it. Who's this?'

I told him, and where I was.

'What are you doing *there*?' he wanted to know.

'I need to find out a few things.'

Pause. 'Sam's not a villain,' he said.

'Maybe, but somebody around him is – you know it better than anyone – and I want to get to the end of this. Have you slept?'

'Not yet.'

'Go do it. How's your Mom?'

'Not in danger, they say.'

'Not at the moment. Good.'

'What do you mean "not at the moment"?'

He had that flick of a challenge I'd noted at first. 'I'll get to that after I've prevented it,' was my answer. 'What I need from you now is the entry-code to PROIE. You do have it, don't you?'

Was there hesitation? Did he wonder about me? No reason not to. Still, he gave it – you have to trust somebody; instinct. He'd wanted to trust Sam. He'd put faith in that relation, and you could hardly blame him. But was it sound? Rafe was young. 'San' had been a mascot, cultivated for a purpose, malign possibly. Did the boy – no, young man, because that's what he was, or would be – have the insight to see through a snow-job? Would I have had at his age? an age when we all long to run with the tough boys? Possibly. In any event he'd transferred the surrogate dad or big brother rôle onto me, so it was up to me to protect him and do so better than I had the first time.

Going back to the building, I slipped along its smooth walls and found a dial-pad recessed on the far side of raised letters. I punched in the code and pressed at the door. It moved open.

Someone was inside – you could feel, smell it on the swish of released air. Sensation came on you like an eddy of musk through the dark – near ebony, like the skin of the Nubians Leni Riefenstahl fell in with after her Aryan passion had gone up in flame. Across black fell a glint like the flash of a knife-blade. One long rent of pallor cut from the room Mazandaran had sat in with designers and thugs. I slipped off my loafers – time for silence, not fashion. Slipped off my socks too – the floor was polished concrete. Like a panther or lynx, I went – OK, let's not get fancy. But I was hyper-aware: how could you not be in that space where the shadows your eyes strained to peer through were meant to seduce you into a chthonic jungle fantasy?

'Yes?' – It was *her* voice, the rich alto. 'And where are you now?... No, I'm in St Tropez... Yes, precisely... No, they've been let go... Yes, I think... My dear, I can't say; I don't want you involved... No, *you* mustn't be; *them* I don't care about, you can get others... Anywhere. Arabs, Africans. Do you have any idea what people like that cost in Marrakech or Algiers?... Well, you're in France now; don't take them, it's simple... How's the girl?... Yes, I see. Well, try not to lose your head.' – She laughed: a low gurgle, simple, friendly. 'And your dear mama?... Good, good. Until then... I will. Bye lovey, bye.'

By now I was next to the office and could see through its door: an inch of table, a chair, the map on the wall, but no her. Receiver clicking, there was no more sound. I held my breath. Then it came up again: hesitation; then back down. Who would she have been trying to phone a second time? Why did she stop? My guess would be answered when her erstwhile accomplices showed. Meanwhile, she must have worked out that police would be listening in on their phones.

Had they been released then? It was Dewey and José surely, maybe others. Her 'nephew' had lent them – aren't families sweet? But she'd kept what she wanted a degree separate from him – 'mustn't be implicated'. That was something: she felt something for someone; many perhaps. But how could you enter her psyche? What did I know of her truly? 'The body of a sixteen year old'? So she had said. Now I heard something further – new sound from that room... She was weeping. 'Oh why, why, why?' – That's how it began. 'Oh why, why, why?'

These may not be the words exactly, but it's what they sounded like. And they kept coming, in susurrus, crescendo-ing in that remarkable alto – 'Why, why, why?... Oh why, why, why?'

Why indeed?

I waited. The sound didn't stop. With it came rocking – you could see her shadow via the crack of the door. It grew bigger, then smaller; then something happened. Exactly what wasn't clear at first, but shortly I realized that she'd climbed up on the table.

Light from below cast her shape on the wall, wavering, dark, ghastly, monstrous. 'Why, why, why?' the sound went, followed by a clang – bracelet being tossed down. Next came a dull thud – some stripped-off piece of clothing. 'Why, why, why' transformed into a shrill ululation, until she had become something other, a shape shifting in serpentine twists. At last the door opened; light poured into that space, concentrating in a beam against the jungle tree, spoking via its branches into long, uncanny streams. Out she slunk.

She seemed wholly mindless that anyone might be there. Creeping like a cat or a lynx, or sliding like that snake, she seemed at the same time to be the Bonnard nude precisely and its obverse. Agèd, wretched, physically haggard, she was free of every one of these qualities too, beneath or beyond them, still an embodiment of a sixteen-year-old – pale, orderly, virtuous, even precious and eminently *violable*. 'Why, why, why? Oh, oh, oh…'

She scampered off to the shadows, twisted, danced, seemed to whirl, letting out whoops. She shrieked and broke wind; cackled and cried; disappeared by the tree, reappeared on a branch, climbed – at which point I stepped into the light, and she stopped dead.

'Who's there?' she demanded, alto cracking.

I gave no answer. I must have appeared no more than a silhouette to her. 'Qui est là?

I stepped forward, out of the light.

She had crouched. Neither of us could see the other. Was I a dream to her? hallucination?

'Qui est là? – Who's there?'

I said no word, made no sound. She was not near any light-switch, nor in that place would it have been less than some state-of-the-art gizmo that took two techies to turn on. Well, we would get them; but not yet. I'd be behind the trunk myself when they stepped in. Her?

Determined or careless, she restarted her dance, this time with something more deliberate about it, as if a performance – the swirling of a dervish, though I'd never seen one; ritual steps of a shaman. I was put in mind of some girl at an acid-test when I'd been young, hippy chick off her head in Californian ecstasy. 'Oh why, why, why?' The words dissolved into sing-song, gave way to new ululation. Sometimes she grew visible through bushes and rocks; other times she was subsumed by the thickets. Swirling out suddenly, as if seductive, she would prance through the light, then slink back like a leper, as if scared or ashamed. Mostly though, she just showed herself wild and angry; triumphant with rage, livid, challenging God to be dead.

Well, He delivered, you might say. Because as she ranted, I heard the heavy doors behind me click and half-turned to see two larger shadows loom in.

She must not have noticed, because when they flipped on the whole jamboree of *son et lumière,* she was writhing stark naked over parquet, face down, head covered by hair, fists pounding and voice wailing, 'Why, why, why?... O no, no, no!'

'Far out, man!' I heard the surfer cluck as he and his partner froze, more shocked by what they saw than *it* was by the upsurge of purples and greens and sounds of jungle beasts wired to shunk on with them; of animal cries and bird screeches – the whole stupefying, ersatz-primitive world, so oddly gorgeous and compelling. It could have been no more than three seconds, this phase of stopped time. Then 'Far out, man!' came again, and from the Chicano, 'Let's do it!' And what would follow would be more than a vision of the grotesque.

You could only think, if you could, that whatever she'd done could never have merited this. But every move that came now arrived at such speed that none seemed to have the remotest connection to thought. And even to try to describe what happened then feels like attempting to cram an aeon into seconds – so I won't. How could you? And no doubt it's obvious enough.

They chased her. I needed to get to a phone – what could one thin man do to stop this on his own?

Her body slithered back to the dark. It was half rising by the time they caught up to it. She was moaning and screeching; or was that the sound howling down off the tape? Whatever. Wild drum-beats were part of it, flares of light as if to announce thunder, gusting wind. All this might've been mildly atmospheric, but then came the shrieks – of madness, panic, fear and shame, what? Here was a body being swirled down to Hell, until a last cry penetrated all other sounds and died off, then rose again – 'Murderers! Assassins! My son, you *killed* him! killed him! Murderers! Fools! Incompetents!'

So it went.

'Chinga!' I heard and saw half in shadow them do what they did. She wailed 'Murderers! Assassins!' on and on, on and on, until it became less articulate, muffled, increasingly distant; and they went at her, grimacing, laughing, swearing both 'Chinga' and 'Fuck' from two sides, without a scintilla of care as to whether she were sixteen or sixty, human or sub, female or male, animal, living or dead. It was de Sade and no other, laced with racist, sexist, brute malice; and always 'My son, you killed him! Murderers! Assassins!' on and on, prickling my hairs as I stood in the door of the box-room trying to lift a receiver. Before I could dial, all sound had been topped by two articulate cracks. And I looked back to see Sam Mazandaran step in the heavy doors, cross the space and fire a pistol at Dewey and José.

Seeing my shadow, he glanced over – 'Call police!' Lowly a gurgle came from her direction, a moan out from under unabating sounds. José had been hit and was staggering into a patch of dark; Mazandaran finished him with one more report. Dewey, stupefied, was tripping over his pants at the ankles; Mazandaran ended his fun with two more – 'Die, fucker. Die!' There was no time or need to phone anyone. As Zabiha emitted a last splintering groan, others stepped through the doors: Rafe, the detective, Occitan man. Mazandaran was up the slope, half in beam, half in black, leaning over her looking like a weird, lumpish cowl kneading a quivering, split-open gourd of red, white and flesh – a *thing* that seemed to deliquesce in his hands.

I walked past the others where they stood frozen. Stepping out to an edge of the parking-lot, I retched. Bringing my head up, I put it back down to vomit another stream, then another, then one more… All was silent. Sound cut off inside while out here, pulled up next to two vulture Alfas, sat a new Maserati. From its dim interior you just could make out the eyes of the actress. As I focused, they turned away.

'Me, I was part of the nastiness now,' an author had once ven-triloquized for Dad. Now I was initiated into the sensation. I didn't like myself much, or was tempted not to. I didn't care for something inside me, or was it outside? But what was it exactly? And was it in me only, or in every one of us?

There aren't many places to run to when you begin to feel prevarication all around. But when you get to my age, you may start to experience this general drift, this edging towards borders of an indifference that the world should be as it is. Observation clicks in, that comforting tourist mode; relaxation into cheery contemplativeness, masquerading as some kind of Buddhistic serenity. You don't want to fall into this fully: if you're honest with yourself, a few dark nights of the soul will tell you you're in danger of entering the Big Sleep of not caring. To be a voyeur *tout court* may strike you as more or less to neuter yourself. Still, you're tugged by an idea that – if you don't draw back a little and accept what's on offer – you may not be able to carry on in any sensible way. You may become one of those failed actors who's a danger to himself at the least, if not everyone else.

I spent some time trying to collate the stray bits of her career and piece them together. She'd come from the East, trailing Scheherazade dreams of a thousand and one nights in the West. In her young eyes the lights of crepuscular dawns danced, tableaux of romantic adventure. Naïve from the start, she was homesick and ill-prepared for the types of hard joy and genital materialism she would encounter in Sartrean Paris and pre-punk London. A chicken among hawks, *petite* songbird underneath big birds of prey, she failed to grasp what an exotic allure she could have. And it would be fatal for her.

Alexandra in particular had been mesmerized – the innocence, delicacy, attributes that gaudy top model, *belle laide* as she was, had no trace of in herself. She was the one who had brought the little *oiseau* into 'the scene'. Her playwright husband, more intrigued by an undercurrent of homoerotic longing than any biological urge for a child, encouraged the affection. He bought her the Bonnard because, as she said at a preview at Christie's, 'It's just like Zabiha!' Indeed, it was precisely Zabiha as she'd appeared to the girls the first time they could catch her, undress her and play at making her over into a version of what they already were. So a shy and pure child of the East was initiated into new Western ways. Not long after came the moment Liskau described; the terrible thing happened, and history changed.

'So,' I put to him the week following her savage *finis*, 'the neo-con boy was her son?' – We were on The Rock again, in front of that view as pristine as an étude by Debussy.

'My dear, she adored him…' Not so crude as to appear glib, he gazed into far azure. 'It had to be hush-hush. In her naïve state she did not recognize her condition, or admit it to herself, until too late. As for her parents in Beirut… can you imagine how people like that might react to news that their daughter was to be a single mother, and under such circumstances? It was enough that her sister had married a Jew, Persian albeit, and moved to the land of the Great Satan.'

She had gone to the country to give birth, a cottage in Wiltshire arranged by Edward – surprising you may think, but Edward proved 'a brick', whereas Luther, the biological father, simply went to ground, to be paid back by his stroke later. Whether out of shame at his friend's behaviour or guilt over the woman's fate, Edward offered protection. He put out a story that she'd gone to work on a memoir about girlhood in Lebanon which a publishing friend had commissioned. Later he brought the child into his home, later still got him into prep school, then Harrow, then Oxford; thus Zabiha's evident, otherwise inexplicable devotion to him. In time he would help her publish a memoir, to favourable reviews extracted from colleagues. On the strength of it, she went on to write travel pieces for the broadsheets he worked for, which kept her in funds. Alexandra and her husband did not neglect her either. She became 'part of the family' each Christmas in the Var and on summer outings. Her secret was safe – that is, the one they knew about. But there was another that none of them had access to or suspected: the hatred she harboured, passion to be avenged, wild fury tucked up in the innards of a soul too shrewd not to appear genial, join in and *pretend*, while plotting every step of the way.

This was the story told me by Liskau. Alexandra and Edward put something similar to Rafe. We were meant to agree more or less on what had happened and the implications of it, which were anyhow impossible to negate – i.e., that Zabiha had prevailed on her nephew's thugs to commit arson but that the operation had been too successful, engulfing at least one party it hadn't been meant for. Who could've guessed that that neo-con boy, having grown up either neuter or gay so far as the world knew, would have gone off with the girls for a frolic? Had some streak of his father's, an identity he had never known, suddenly surfaced? Other questions burbled up, such as Edward's knowledge or not of what was afoot; his suspicions and fortuitous escape from a fate met by almost every other original sinner. That was odd; Alexandra's survival too. Nor might it have failed to strike a jaundiced observer that there could be other motives or connections more deeply buried in what we saw, which happened to be what *they* wanted us to see and applied subtle suasion to make sure we accepted.

Their version extended further, to explain how Alexandra had been poisoned. Zabiha, it was claimed, had sent her a box of figs from Beirut, which she had taken to Genoa on that visit to Liskau's, but only opened once she and Edward had been en route back to the Var. To a sceptic, this might have sounded fortuitous. But it was among 'the facts' that soon solidified.

The police were persuaded to adopt them, after some hesitation. The Muslim terrorist angle hardly suited them, but in due course they agreed to withdraw their tale about development in the Var and re-brand the crime as ancient, personal, *passionel* – a weird saga of revenge. They gave Mazandaran a rough week. It beggared belief that his Deweys and Josés could have been used by Zabiha without his knowledge or tacit assent; it also seemed more than by chance that he should have shown up just in time to finish them off before they could breathe a word of confession. But that could be spun as *passionel* too – Zabiha was his aunt, so said, thus the neo-con boy his cousin. And the police may have had another concern: fear of being accused of being too loose in releasing the tough guys so soon after inconclusive investigation of Rafe's misadventure below Bonne Terrasse. In the end I suspect, and Liskau intimated, what motivated them most was to not shoot themselves in the foot. They might close down PROIE, but why act against a high-profile foreigner like Mazandaran, unless they had an open-and-shut case? He lived with an actress who was headlines at Cannes; he'd bring trailing investment if he set up here; so why not pretend he was a 'friend' and trustworthy? Why not give him an incentive – indeed, compulsion – not to pick up his toys and run back to the no-longer quite so mean streets of West L.A.?

So life returned to normal, if you could call it that. But it was a normal in which all the pieces had shifted slightly and not quite spokenly. And this unspokenness, in fact, was essential; because underneath it you might have heard a faint whisper that something had been going on that wasn't any more, some larger plot which – having reached an impasse – had been put on hold for a time. And if this were so, you might be tempted to add that some good had come out of that brutal last scene in 'the jungle'. Whatever nefarious dealings had been afoot were suspended, so that for now there would be no more cars filled with ammonium nitrate or whatever, no more arson attacks, no more nervy escapes into the middle of the deep blue.

Loretta and James could return to Liskau: something was worked out there that would be half explained in due course; meanwhile, as the designer laboured over a wedding frock for an actress, they could sail his yacht between Santa Margherita and Cannes, leaving the Timer's tub again in Villefranche for its interrupted repairs. Rafe stayed with his mother, and before long the two of them were back in the Var, he to supervise renovations on the half-ruin, which they seemed content to leave in its half-state, as if an emblem for the half-certain world we all now existed in. I had a half-burnt face – did I want surgery on it? no time soon: 'gals like rough'. There were half-solved crimes out there – did the authorities want to wrap them up? not with speed evidently. There were twin brothers, one half-Caliban, half-Ariel, who were my half brothers, or may have been, along with another brother and/or sister. Did I want to find out? test DNA? or could we all dwell in the half-uncertainties we apparently shared, the half-nationalities, bi-sexualities, half-puritan/half-licentious personalities that seemed to belong to most, if not all, of us. Nothing was black and white here, nothing bell clear. So I observed, or complained, to Liskau. To which he retorted, sitting at his perch on that terrace gazing out towards a pearl-grey band of incoming cloud,

159

'My dear, this is Europe. The story is long. Things may get worked out for a time, more or less. They rarely get solved finally.'

So it was, Dad. In high summer an actress and her nightclub suitor got married. There was a gala bash atop the Rock: paparazzi had employment; GL's rococo gown was splashed over the covers of *Hello* and *Grazia* or whatever those rags call themselves; the glitz world made a glam Riviera shine once again in new permutation of the old formula – Grace and Ranier, *haute culture* and fizz, the dark and the zazzy. Then, some months later, just before Alexandra and Rafe had assigned a tranche of their land to an elaborate development scheme, the actress became cover-girl in GL again, this time heavily pregnant; and the maternity outfits she would model were soon setting a tone for a trend to rage under the label 'Maman chic'.

Whose baby was it? I wondered, naturally. And who, if Alexandra, Rafe and Jimmy were all of a sudden whisked off in some *crise,* would stand to inherit potential millions? She was wealthy, the actress, so why should she care? So too her husband, so why 'look under toadstools'? As to those who might've been able to blackmail them... the factotum was gone; Loretta seemed happy; and me – ?

I loitered in a café in San Raphaël, pondering on when or whether I should go up to Nice to pick up my passport. Beyond that, I was trying to work out the character of an elegant, yet subtly twisted individual like Giovanni Liskau. I was still doing so a month or two later when *Var-Matin* ran a piece about an American nightclub owner who had fallen twenty storeys to his death from a Monaco balcony. His widow, a world-famous actress, was 'shattered'. It was 'a tragedy', and not least because a few weeks earlier their so looked-forward-to baby had succumbed to cot-death.

That fact hadn't been reported at the time. Why?

Wouldn't you wonder?

Some time later, as I sat ruing the fate of so many of my countrymen from a mould Dad had thrived in, I found myself half-worrying, not a little curiously, about who out in that vast unknown I was facing might have been comforting her.

– London, Bad Wiessee, 2006 and after